the Pilgrim's Ladder

The Pilgrim's Ladder

Ryan D. Montoya

ISBN-13: 978-1542737906

ISBN-10: 1542737907

First Printing: 2017

Illustrations by Ciara Kay Barsotti

DEDICATION

To my Grandfather,
Who inspired me to write, and to live boldly
in both mind and body.

ACKNOWLEDGEMENTS

I want to thank my sister, for her beautiful pieces of art that she generously designed for my novel. I also want to thank my mother and father, for the long hours of proofreading, and discussion they provided. Many of the core ideas of this book would not have been developed without both of you.

I. the Valley

WONDER

In the early seasons of youth, a child is carefully fed morsels of reality. As the child grows, so does his appetite. The world preprocessed into a benign substance soon fails to satisfy, and the child begins to search for further nourishment. Unfiltered reality leaks through the carefully constructed shroud that encompasses all the child knows. But the shroud is finite, and as the mind wanders it becomes entangled in its folds. Claustrophobia inspires reaction, and in a flash the curtain is pulled away.

A young mind lay awake in the late hours of the night, bundled tightly in a coarse woolen blanket. His breath crystalized in the falling temperature, and a draft tickled his body through the weaknesses of his fabric cocoon. The boy was unresponsive, despite the growing cold. He lay stiff; his hands clutched his blanket and his gaze was unbroken.

The boy and his bed were swallowed by darkness, but the light of his thought flickered before his eyes. Out of the blackness a sparkling, unbroken rampart of pinnacles and spires towered above him. Each high summit donned a gleaming cap of permafrost, their corniced ridges bending ominously over abysses of rock and ice. A high gust was evident on the proudest of these spires as loose snow escaped on glittering tendrils across the sky.

The boy had seen this mighty range before, both in his dreams and with his waking eyes. The range instilled a deep fear in the boy's heart, a cold claw that threatened his very pulse. What the boy feared he did not yet understand, but he knew the object of his terror was hidden in the bosom of the mountains.

In the inky blackness the white summits stood illuminated by a celestial glow, the source of which seemed to emanate from the boy himself. But to the boy's surprise he suddenly noticed an almost imperceptible light that strobed beyond the broken teeth of the range. His absent gaze fractured;

unfocused eyes were drawn tightly to the origin. The light was faint at first, but grew in intensity. Unknown to the boy, as soon as his eyes met with the anomaly an ember settled into his chest and burst into flame.

The smoldering heat softened the grip on his heart and beat itself steadily along the passages of his veins. With every inch the thaw was accompanied by a distant thrum, once soft but now growing steadily. The boy felt it in the air, in his bones, and finally in his ears. As the warmth progressed the thrum began to saturate the landscape. The mountains shook off their corniced shoulders, sending tons of ice plummeting into the void with a snap followed by a whisper. A strong glow was now evident on the horizon, urged on by the rising anthem. The gaunt trees that dotted the landscape dropped their white coats and greedily stretched their fingers in the rising light. The boy felt the warmth tingling in his fingers, and with a final mighty thrum the grip on his heart was shattered.

At once the landscape was still.

CURIOSITY

When the world reveals itself, it is naturally inviting to the curious few. The earth becomes a playground with marvelously hidden pearls of truth. Most children will focus on the objects of grandeur, and yet a minority partakes in a more studious inquiry. Driven by wonder, the child takes a stick and begins turning over stones; little does he know that unsightly creatures hide in the shadows.

Dawn beckoned the denizens of the valley to emerge from their shelters. Long fields of grass rippled and waved in the changing winds, and the smell of pollen and dirt rode the air. With short breath a youth sampled the wind, all in stride. She walked quickly and with intention through a trail flattened over the seasons by the passage of livestock. Her heel dipped into a collection of dew and evening rainwater; her dress stood as a muddy testament to the occurrence of such collections. Her golden hair blazed in the orange morning glow.

The trail opened into a small clearing that circumscribed a broad, leafy tree. The base of the tree was fantastically knotted and a singular branch sprouted perpendicular to the trunk from a gruesome twist in the wood. The branch, though it had begun life in effort to join the canopy above, soon bent low under the weight of its own endeavor and grazed the soil at its terminus. At this intersection the branch again turned skyward, and as consequence formed a comfortable saddle. A boy sat on this saddle. His heels dug into the dirt below, and his little shoulders sagged easily at his sides.

"Looking at them again, Micah?" The girl wondered aloud as she took a seat beside him.

"Yes." The boy let slip from his lips. He did not acknowledge her presence except for this single word. She looked at him curiously for a moment, and then turned away. Her eyes followed his own and swept out over the vast plain before them. The land stretched for countless miles, basking in the light of the flowering sunrise. Small wooden cottages dotted the valley, and as the sun rose their furnaces coughed up flames. From rusting chimney pipes wisps of smoke were tugged along by the prevailing breeze.

Micah did not see the valley laid plain before him. His eyes traversed past sleepy households, livestock, and billowing meadows alike, finally coming to rest on a distant horizon. Dark clouds lingered at the edge of their world, forming a formidable barrier to the encroaching daylight. There jutted the object of his dreams, a cathedral of cold stone that thrust a thorny crown into the clouds above.

The girl eyed the range with perceptible indifference. "Mama said you should be helping Papa in the morning." Micah offered no response. "She doesn't like you coming out here so often. I don't like it either," she added.

Micah broke his vigil. He dropped his head and managed a smile. "I heard another story last night." His sister snapped to attention and opened her mouth to protest. "I know, but please don't tell Mama," Micah interjected.

His sister frowned but held her tongue momentarily. The pleading note in Micah's voice weakened her resolution. "You shouldn't sneak around that place," she mumbled, knowing that it fell on deaf ears. Micah grinned sheepishly.

"Do you remember the old storyteller that came into town yesterday?"

"Yes," she nodded.

"He says he crossed them." His grin broadened. "He says he saw the other side."

A moment passed, and then another. A field cricket gained the courage to infuse the air with a song. Micah's sister fumbled absent-mindedly with a brittle leaf.

"What did he see?" The leaf crumbled in her hands. Micah's smile faltered. Her tone was frustrated, but worst of all to him carried a dull note of defeat.

The fractured leaf spun slowly to the earth. "Nothing." Micah turned his attention once again to the horizon. "Just another valley. One like our own. There was no great city. No marble halls." His voice fell to a whisper. "No prophets and no white gates." His smile had disappeared.

6

"Do you believe him?"

"I don't know. I don't know what to believe. Nobody who has seen it has ever come back. But when someone returns, they claim it doesn't exist. A few men told him he didn't go far enough. That's what they usually say. And why should anyone return who has found it anyway? It has everything we don't." Micah paused for a moment, collecting his thoughts. His words had tumbled out clumsily. His sister bent down to the dirt and carelessly traced an uncertain line through the dirt with her finger.

"So go and ask the Elder. He will explain it." The line faltered. She flashed an encouraging smile. "Your mountains are boring." She dismounted the branch. "I'm going to go and help Mama. You should come home soon." A faint crunching of leaves indicated her retreat down the trail.

Micah sat, pensive. He sighed, swung a leg over the branch, and started for home.

INQUIRY

Among the inquisitive there comes a point in life when all that a young mind has been nurtured on gets called into question. Such a mind, if driven, might choose to unravel these doubts. This pursuit is liable to shake the very foundation of his knowledge. Quickly the once timid question becomes a mountain; few can estimate the magnitude of the endeavor and fewer still choose to accept the quest. Most often a seeker will idly toy with their new thread until the entire fabric collapses.

It was dusk by the time Micah had finished his daily work. He stood in the field, watching his father round up the livestock. His father cut a striking contrast in the falling light. A cloudless day was slowly devoured by the ensuing night leaving a gradient of blacks and blues that echoed across the heavens.

The goats protested Micah's weak hand, but hurried to obey his father's. Micah relinquished his lead to his father and watched as the stock was expertly corralled into the fenced enclosure adjacent to their little home. Their cottage was modest, like all in the valley. It contained a small room for Micah, a similar room for his sister, a room for their father and mother, and a common room with a wood stove. Smoke trailed lazily from the stove pipe, and Micah caught the scent of boiled lamb with a trace of herbal seasoning picked from the garden. His stomach rumbled in anticipation.

A click announced the closure of the gate, and the end of another day of work. Micah's father turned towards their home, wiping his hands on his burlap trousers.

"Papa!" Micah called out. His father continued walking but gave Micah a curious look.

"Yes Micah?"

"Would Mama be upset if I missed supper? I think I left my knife down by the tree."

"No Micah, I think that would be alright. Don't stay out too late." His father arrived at their front door, and with a firm grip swung the door open wide. An orange light flickered inside. Micah almost took a step forward, driven by his gurgling appetite, but remembered himself and solemnly watched as his father let the door pivot shut in his wake.

The full moon now reigned in the sky. A dirt road parted a broiling sea of tall grass that shimmered under a white nocturnal glow. The road ran directly north to the horizon, surrounded by a forest of blades. Micah had walked this road many times. The remoteness and linearity of the road was commonly the object of his amusement as he travelled. Micah would direct himself to the center, close his eyes, and walk for as long as he could before he inevitably stumbled into the adjacent drainage. He walked slowly, reflecting on his day. Micah regretted lying to his father, but he did not want to arouse suspicion and so felt confident that his decision was necessary.

Something beside the road suddenly caught his foot midstride, rousing him from the depths of introspection and introduced him to the bottom of the ditch. His eyes snapped open just moments before impacting the muddy soil. Filthy but unhurt, Micah clambered out of the ditch and struggled to wipe earthy remnants from his clothing. Realizing its futility, he dropped his hands to his sides and made note of his surroundings.

The road still ran straight as an arrow, and the moon now shone directly overhead. From just above the tall grass, a small hill could be seen illuminated in the distance. On this hill was built a lonely clay hut, more modest than even Micah's home. The hut belonged to the Elder of the valley. It was here that Micah intended to seek answers to his ravenous curiosity. Forgetting entirely about the state of his appearance, Micah eagerly set off for the hill at a doubled pace. He had never visited the Elder before, but his opinion was greatly valued by the entire community. He felt certain that he would know what lay beyond The Divide.

The door to the hut was as modest as the rest of the structure. It was so short that an ordinary adult would be forced to stoop; however, it was quite naturally sized to Micah's stature. The door had been fashioned out of seasoned birch limbs woven together with grass fibers. Clay had been used to seal the limbs together and protect against the winter cold, and over time rot that had set in to the birch had been patched with additional clay. For it was time and poverty that had transfigured the door and the majority of the residence from wood into mud. The structure, despite a lack of proper building materials, had been carefully maintained, and was well equipped against even the most bitter of winters.

Micah stood nervously at the door, uncertain of how to proceed. He knew very little about the man that lived inside, and was not even certain that the man was home. No smoke rose from the little iron chimney that broke from the mold, and there was no light visible from around the seams of the door. The door which had at first seemed so insignificant to Micah now rose as a formidable barrier. Working up his courage into a little fist, Micah dared to rap his knuckles on the old earthen frame. He waited expectantly, but his announcement was met with no answer. After a long moment of restraint, Micah's fear was replaced with irritation. His groaning stomach prompted him to regret his decision to forego a hot meal, and his face glowed red as he was confronted with his own supposed naivety. His fist steeled, and he gave the door a single, forceful knock.

"Be careful my son, for that door is older than you are."

The voice leapt at Micah from behind, causing him to start violently. He whirled around to confront its owner. On the path that led to the humble abode stood a stooping figure bundled tightly in a tattered sheepskin cloak. The figure toted a pack of firewood sticks, and seemed to totter under the insignificant load.

"Now, what is it that I can do for you?" His voice was light and inviting, but age permeated his speech like the creaking of boughs. Micah's mouth had run dry from his sudden panic; he struggled to form any words. The old man waited patiently as Micah clumsily formed an explanation.

"I am looking for the Elder who lives here," Micah finally managed. The old man raised a bushy white eyebrow. "You are the Elder?"

"That is what they call me." The Elder offered a taut smile, collecting the wrinkles of his face into stiff bunches. "Though I question if the title is earned by form or by merit!" Micah's blank expression begged further explanation, which the Elder casually avoided. "Tell me, why is it that you have come here so late in the evening? Surely this visit could have waited until daylight. I am old, and must rest before the morning harvest. And you are only a child, you should be home with your parents!"

"But sir, I have an inquiry that has been foremost on my mind," Micah blurted. He had rehearsed his question countless times that evening, maximizing his vocabulary in an effort to conceal youthfulness. The effect was remarkably counterproductive as his tongue stumbled on the unfamiliar sounds. Realizing this, his speech collapsed midstride, and his face reddened once more.

The Elder's expression softened. "Do not worry, for your question is important to me. I hope it is one that I can answer."

Hearing this, Micah's heart skipped. He mustered his confidence and tried again. "Sir, what I want to know is, what lies beyond the Northern Divide?"

The Elder listened attentively, but to Micah's dismay released a slight chuckle. Micah flushed, painfully aware of the nature of his question. A smile lingered on the Elder's face, and he turned, bringing the north into his field of view. The range was invisible under a heavy layer of clouds. Across the horizon flashes of brilliant light split the night sky, and the occasional toothy silhouette bit through the blackened clouds by a momentary aura of white.

The Elder did not break his gaze with the horizon. "My son, you could tell me what lies beyond those mountains."

"But sir, I don't believe it," Micah pleaded. "My parents told me the stories of the City of the Gods, just like their parents did them. They told me about the great wonders, about the great Kings and Queens, about the white cloaks and their strange medicine. They told me about the Library of the Ages, and of its guardians: the keepers of its knowledge. I know of the temple, visited by the gods themselves; I have heard it all!"

"Then why do you not believe them?"

Micah's frustration rose. "Because none of them have seen it! And of the travelers who have returned, some say that it does not exist! They say that there is nothing, nothing but another valley!" Micah appended a hasty "Sir," in effort to maintain some vestige of civility.

"You should be wary of the tavern folk; it is not a place for children." The Elder remained fixed on the horizon. Micah was taken aback, and mumbled a weak apology. The Elder ignored him, but returned his sharp, dark eyes to Micah's. "Perhaps they have not gone far enough?" He smiled.

Micah evaded the question. Instead, he asked in desperation, "Have you ever been across The Divide?"

The Elder's smile faded. "My child, in my youth I traveled far, I saw many lands pass beneath my feet. Of the men in the mountains, I had no equal." The elder's eyes were a dull grey in the moonlight. "I have seen much child, but what would it mean to you to hear of the lands that I saw? You, who has already heard so much, but seen so little. What are an old man's words to such youth?"

At this Micah's already dwindling hopes were snuffed by frustration. He stuffed his hands in his pockets, and muttered a polite yet brisk thanks to the Elder. Without another word Micah started down the path home. But before he could get more than a few paces down the trail, the Elder's voice halted him.

"Stop! My child, I am sorry for not understanding. Though you are young, you have a lifetime ahead of you. Perhaps in time you will see. But if my age and long wandering have given me wisdom, it is that such questions must be answered. Do not deny them, do not ignore them. If they call you to go far, if they call you to strange and fearsome places, then listen. But still you are young, your guide is not true. Beware the long journey, beware The Divide. Though along it you may find your answer, remember that by pain are its answers revealed. Remember this if your passion takes you there, and remember that not only by its trail might the City be found. If you are careful, if you are wise, then you might find the answers much closer to your heart. For your sake child, I hope that you do."

The Elder clasped his hands, and the pale moon revealed that he wore a pained expression. He stood next to his simple home, and in that moment seemed to wither beside it. Micah, not knowing how to respond, nodded again to the Elder in thanks and then turned once more for home.

That evening was the last anyone of the valley saw the Elder. Days passed, then weeks, and rumor of his absence spread. A month passed and the crumbling home began to sprout weeds. In less than a year the home left abandoned on its lonely hillside had rejoined the soil, and the Elder was seldom spoken of again.

INSPIRATION

While the mind of the youth is free to probe life's mysteries, an adult must reconcile the fantastic with the absolute contrast of physical reality. A young adult faced with such a dichotomy will often manage them poorly and side with an extreme. Those tending towards responsibility take a firm stance in practicality. The fantastic is reduced to a playground for the young; necessities such as primitive survival become distinct priorities. But the curious: the few who uncovered life's greatest wonders while their peers satisfied themselves with oddities, these few can never forget the significance of what they had uncovered.

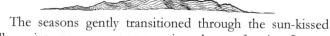

The seasons gently transitioned through the sun-kissed valley; winter gave way to a transitory burst of spring flowers which immediately surrendered to the slow burn of the summer. Fall then stole through on its toes, and craftily swapped summer with winter. Every iteration behaved identically to its predecessor; however, to Micah the seasons seemed to creep faster with every passing.

Micah was now a young man, and carried the responsibilities that his title earned. He was learning the trade of his father, destined to carry on the homestead for another generation. His once soft hands grew calloused and hard; his father no longer handled the herd. His father was growing old, and needed to rest frequently from the long days in the field. Micah loved his father very much, and found purpose in saving him from labor.

But Micah held no special love for his work in itself. In it, his mind was kept forever busy, and over the seasons an unsettling feeling of neglect crept over him. The local tavern he once visited as a child became a frequent respite; Micah was not fond of abusing the local ales but he did value the emptiness of mind that accompanied it.

Evening in the pub was generally quiet but on occasion the local farmhands would gather to share stories. If ever a traveler spent the day in the little village, they found the shepherds and goatherds there quite apt at their profession and were ushered into the tavern to recollect tales of past adventures, encounters, and of life beyond the valley. The locals were greedy to live a day, if vicariously, in another part of the world they knew so little about. As a child Micah was captivated by such tales, but as the seasons slipped by the enchantment had begun to slip.

The tavern was dimly lit by a multitude of wax candles. Micah sat in a corner, nursing an ale and allowing his mind to clear. Only a handful of men and women were sprinkled about, most sat quietly as Micah did and enjoyed the stillness. A few conversed, and a pair played a game of dice. The murmur was agreeable, however, and Micah noticed his eyelids grow heavy. He was very nearly asleep when a husky voice boomed out from the beyond the tavern door.

"Come now sir, you cannot refuse a drink with us! It simply isn't proper to begin business without having a drink to correct the senses! And wouldn't you know it, you certainly have a trifle or two, where have you come by all of it?"

With a crash the front door was flung open and a party of four rushed inside in perfect formation. At their epicenter a wide-eyed, dirty looking man gave the appearance of being forcibly shepherded inside. Each of his escorts gripped the man and eagerly led him to the bar. Micah speculated that if the man were to simply raise his feet that he would stay suspended by their arms. The men soon arrived at their destination and helped the newcomer into a stool. The moment the man opened his mouth he tasted ale, and he was not allowed to speak until he had polished off a pint, most of which collected in his scraggly beard.

The man sported a large rucksack filled with his wares. With the help of his new companions this was set aside so that the gaggle could surround him more closely. They crowded him, laughing and making jokes while they waited for the bartender to fill their cups. The newcomer was visibly uncomfortable, and kept a nervous eye on his goods. But as the ale continued to pour he gradually eased into his stool and engaged in the conversation. His voice was shrill, and grew in

15

volume proportionally to the number of empty cups on the counter.

"So my new friend," rumbled the same thick voice that had broken the quiet evening, "where have you come from? You don't look to be from around here."

The man opened his mouth to speak but was interrupted by another of his entertainers, a young goatherd Micah knew by the name of Edgar. "I'll bet he's from across the watershed out east, aren't you?"

"Are you mad? Look at him, he hails from the west, you can tell it by his dress," another local pointed at the traveler's greasy tunic with a laugh.

"I'll have you know I am not from either of those lowly places," the man squeaked before another could interrupt. "I have traveled from lands none of you have ever seen before, or ever will! I speak of course, of beyond The Divide."

His words took a moment to settle into the inebriated audience, but when they did he had their rapt attention. Questions flowed faster than ale, and the herders forgot their easy wit. The entire tavern now watched the man, including Micah. A familiar tug pulled at his conscience. Though he tried to appear disinterested as he previously was, his now motionless posture betrayed him.

The man's eyes bulged with pleasure, and he acknowledged the barrage of questions with a raised hand. His audience quieted. "Yes, from beyond The Divide. I come from the City of the Gods, which all of you no doubt has heard of," he said with satisfaction. "I have made the crossing of The Divide alone, and by my own power of will survived its harshest winter."

"I doubt that very much," interjected the owner of the rumbling voice. "Those mountains have claimed men far stronger than you." He said this pointedly and without a hint of humor.

The oily traveler flared up in indignation, and leapt from his stool. He was small in stature, and was dwarfed by his accuser who stood several hands taller and supported a broad, muscular frame. But he was not about to relinquish his audience or his assumed dignity. With a snarl he pushed a knobby finger into the other man's chest. "You dare question my honor?" He spoke with such fervor that he produced a fine cloud of spit, causing the taller man to step backwards in surprise. In fact, the entire congregation was taken aback by the violent response. Silence followed, uncertain glances were exchanged between farmhands, but the man's eyes remained aggressively fixed on his opponent.

"I do not blame you; it is a feat that very few might suppose to accomplish," the man said, letting his voice drain of its sudden vehemence. He dropped his hand, and eased himself over to his rucksack. "But if you have any doubts my friends, please answer them by taking a quick look into my wares!"

The rucksack containing his goods was opened, and in a transformation as sudden as the man's temper he was configured into the very picture of a traveling entrepreneur. "Please, ladies and gentlemen alike, see the goods available only from beyond The Divide, from the very City of the Gods! I come bringing the tools and knowledge of a civilization far more advanced than your imaginations could possibly conceive! Allow me to open your eyes to technologies that could save the sick and instantly accomplish the work of a hundred days!"

He bent over his sack, and procured a curious vial containing a cloudy solution. "See the tonic that will stop aging- that will bring youth to an elderly face!" He drank in the audience's astonishment, and let the vial dance before their eyes in the candlelight before withdrawing it into his trove. "See the magic powder that can move a mountain, but only if you choose! Again, you do not believe me?" He eyed the tall man mischievously. "Tell me, if you will not believe my words, will you believe your own two eyes?" With a flourish he swept a candle up from the counter and touched the flame to a little brown pouch he had produced from his sack. The pouch exploded with a deafening crack, leaving only a black cloud. Many released an audible scream, and even Micah found himself on his feet after his senses had recovered.

"You see, I tell you all the truth. I have crossed The Divide and returned, and I have been to the City. Now pray tell me, what could you possibly have that I might find a worthy trade for goods such as these?"

The tavern erupted with voices, and even those that previously witnessed from afar joined the circle around the traveler. Livestock, land, favors; the villagers had to beg the traveler to accept their offers. Micah stood at the outside of the group looking in, but the man had disappeared beneath a frantic mass of bodies.

Dusk had long since passed, and a cold darkness permeated the air outside. Grey clouds shrouded the land from the slightest celestial glimmer. Micah waited outside the bustling tavern door. He disliked the commotion inside; however, he felt determined to speak to the traveler and so would not abandon his post. Shivering, he drew his woolen coat higher around his neck, and hugged his body with his arms. One by one the villagers stepped out to return home. Most clutched prizes won from the traveler, and those empty-handed returned with a wondrous story to tell over supper. Micah exchanged brief words with them, many of whom he knew by name. Edgar was one of the last to exit. He exited with a little brown satchel not unlike the one the traveler had used as demonstration. Edgar walked carefully, and held the sack with an outstretched hand. When passing Micah, he refused to take his eyes off of the packet, though he did offer a passing goodbye. Micah watched him walk from the tavern until he was swallowed by the darkness.

At last the tavern was empty but for the bartender and the traveler. Micah proceeded to wait until the man had finished counting his earnings and stepped through the taverns threshold.

"Hello sir, I have not had a moment to ask about your wares!" Micah offered a friendly smile.

The man barely acknowledged his gesture, and continued down the tavern steps. "I'm afraid it's been sold, and I am about to retire." Not about to be dismissed so easily, Micah gained in his footsteps.

"But sir, I must confess that my intention is not to trade. I have questions for you, as someone who has travelled so far and under such circumstances your knowledge is invaluable!"

"You want to hear of my journey across The Divide?"

"Yes, and of the City beyond them! It is really true that you have seen it?"

"Did you see nothing inside, or have you been in the cold all evening?" The man's shrill note adopted an air of irritability, and Micah feared the man's fierce temper was growing.

"Of course, I did see everything! But I wonder if you saw the City itself, or only came by the goods on your travels? I understand that it makes for an excellent story to truly visit the City, and I would not judge you for using that to your advantage." The man stopped abruptly, and cast an ugly look at Micah but said nothing. Micah paused, and then spoke carefully, "But, that would not be agreeable for an honorable man such as yourself."

"I have seen the City, I have entered the City, I even lived in the City," the man sniffed. "Uncountable seasons ago I heard of its magnificence, and I resolved to make the pilgrimage to the marble gates. I was accepted into the halls, and I drank from its holy beauty. The City adopts those who have proven themselves as I had." He added his final statement after a moment of consideration.

A confused look washed over Micah's face. An old question had sprung to mind. The man noticed this, and waited impatiently for it to be asked.

"But sir, if you reached the City of the Gods, why ever did you decide to leave it?" Micah asked slowly.

"A profoundly simple question!" The man exclaimed haughtily. "Why, I had sought my destination and I discovered it! I absorbed its beauty, its essence, and I chose to move on to mightier goals! For what better can a man do than to set and overcome the greatest obstacles these lands have to offer? Boy, if I had not the fortitude of mind that I do possess I could never accomplish all that I have, and what would my life be worth?"

"Remarkable sir," Micah said emphatically. "I have been a farmer's son my whole life, but only now do I feel that I can give words to the nature of my soul! I know that there is more that I can achieve, and my whole body aches for it. Your words are inspiration!" He spoke with passion, and seized the travelers hand in thanks. "Sir, by what name can I call you?"

"My name is Giralt. My words are truth, and you would be wise to adopt them." Giralt's tiny eyes sparkled, and with a puff of his chest drew himself to his full height.

"Thank you, I will not forget it. Giralt, before you leave, please tell me what is it that you have decided to pursue that will triumph even your pilgrimage to the City of the Gods?"

Giralt's smile splintered, and his voice reached an octave previously unknown. "That is not your place to ask, you cannot begin to understand my pursuits until you have surmounted even the smallest mountain of The Divide! And then you will have but a glimpse, so please do not bother me with your questions anymore! I must retire." He peeled his hand from Micah, spun on his heel and marched into the night.

Micah stood alone on the dusty road for some time. What little light that still touched him from the tavern flickered and vanished. He did not feel the cold anymore, and was engaged in a form of meditation he had long since forgotten. A menagerie of emotions danced beside malformed notions; he could not identify each alone, but together they delivered a clear message that even his calloused conscience could not ignore: his soul still wandered north. It drifted lazily along currents of snow under a cerulean sky, emblazoned by the blistering high altitude sun. It drifted over ramparts of stone; over blades of rock and ice that threatened the gods by reaching eagerly into heaven above. His soul floated north into the unknown, yearning for the flash of white marble gates. Micah knew that his soul had left him a long time ago, and that with every passing second it drew further still.

A distant rumble tempted Micah back into reality. Slowly, he lifted his eyes to the source. The gray sky stretched into the farthest reaches of the North, enveloping the world except for a single, solitary peak on the horizon. The dark spire twisted fiercely from a thick harness of cloud, protesting the powers of nature that fought to subdue its wicked ambition. Pelted by sleet and hail, scarred by heaven's repeated strike, the mighty watchtower proudly took vigil, and with an icy lust for blood beckoned daring mortals to attempt its flanks. Micah felt an old fear thicken and freeze the passages of his heart.

CHOICE

The curious few can never abandon the fire which has stolen their soul. For though they might fight to extinguish its flame, the effect is self-destruction. One by one they submit to its pull, knowing fully that it draws them into a place of terror, hardship and insecurity. But these few were never destined to become comfortable. Their call comes from a deeper place: a place of great reward and greater suffering.

After the traveler known as Giralt took leave of the valley, Micah continued to tend to the livestock, but was unable to muster the courage to face his convictions. Instead of seeking solace from his labor, he found himself using it to take refuge from his thought. The very moment he rose from a fitful slumber Micah fled to the fields, and did not return until his body ached and his eyes begged to be shut.

No longer did Micah visit the tavern. The emptiness he found at the bottom of the cup chilled him to the bone. The void yearned to be filled, and though Micah knew what sacrifice was required he was not willing to satisfy it. He came to believe desperately that the objective borne of childhood curiosity was simply that: childhood curiosity, and that the remedy for such a malady could be found in absolute immersion of adult responsibility.

It had been nearly a month since the fateful encounter, and the cold had since released its grip on the valley. Early spring flowers tested the air, and finding it to their satisfaction spread wide under the open sun. The green fields supported brilliant splashes of crimson, lavender and yellow. Despite his developing aversion to absent-mindedness, Micah frequently found himself lost amongst the rippling fields.

In such a moment Micah discovered himself taking careful footsteps on an old, familiar trail. A soft tinkle of bells alerted him to the presence of the herd up the trail amidst the tall grass. Micah followed as it snaked through the fields, leading with a protective hand as the trail was significantly overgrown. The bells led him for some time, and then they stopped. Micah quickened his pace. Rounding a corner, he burst from the thicket and stumbled waist deep into the missing herd. The goats had gathered into a small clearing. Amidst the herd sprouted a wooden growth Micah had frequented as a child, using its knobby limbs to survey the horizon. Upon the bark saddle sat a young woman with golden hair. A slight turn of her head indicated her knowledge of Micah's presence.

"Why don't you look at them anymore?" She faced north.

Micah grimaced, and slowly picked his way through the tangle of goats towards her. Each protested his passage, but then lost interest and returned to grazing.

"I don't need to. There is nothing out there for me, for my life is here." On arriving he took a seat beside her. He offered a smile. She returned the same, but her eyes spoke to another story.

"Micah, if you are home, then why are you not happy?" Her smile faded.

Micah opened his mouth to protest but his sister censured him with a scowl. He blinked, and dropped his eyes to the ground.

"I'm not sure I know," he mumbled. "I've tried so hard, and yet I cannot find my joy. You must think I am ungrateful for our home and family. Perhaps I am." He wrung his hands, and found himself unable to return her gaze.

She did not answer immediately, but instead remained in thought. "Perhaps you are," she agreed finally.

"What can I do Sarah? I have duties, I have responsibility. Our family needs me, and yet my soul aches to depart. Am I wicked for wanting it? Surely it is wrong to be so selfish!" His voice broke with emotion, and he pressed a clenched fist against his forehead. Sarah watched him carefully.

"Would you do it?"

Micah shuddered involuntarily. He shut his eyes tight, and instantly the object of his terror loomed out of the shadows. He stood waist deep in a plain of snow. Wind blasted his face with a million shards of ice and screamed in his ears. The world was white, and the air was thin. No longer could he feel his hands or feet. His knees shook, and collapsed. Micah landed face down in the snow. Within minutes, his body slipped beneath the white blanket.

"No," he whispered.

"Why not?" she replied. Her voice was firm. A note of fire crept into her tone, and her eyes flashed.

"Because it is foolish," he suggested.

"Because you are afraid," she retorted. Micah listened and raised no objection.

"Yes, because I'm afraid." He returned his eyes to hers. They were wide, uncertain and honest. "I'm afraid of what I don't know. I'm afraid of what I will find. I'm afraid I might never return. And I'm afraid to die alone."

Sarah's stern expression softened. "I will never understand why you are drawn to them. Leaving your family, leaving the only people in the world whom you love and who love you back; you are right to think it is foolish." She rested a tender hand on his shoulder. "I love you Micah." She paused. "I don't claim to have answers, because I do not. I wish that I did. But I feel compelled to say that whatever decision you do make, let it not be motivated by your fears."

She rose to her feet, and faced the horizon. "I hope that your love for us is enough to convince yourself otherwise, but if you decide to go, then I will support it."

"But what of the herd Sarah, of Mother and Father? It is not a decision I can make!"

Sarah smiled and shook her head. "I can watch the herd for you. And Mother and Father will never be lonely with me."

"I can't ask you to do that! It is my duty, my responsibility. What kind of man would I be if I abandoned my burden to you?"

"Responsibility and duty," Sarah laughed bitterly. "You talk as if you have lived through forty winters. Micah, I will make this offer only once. Either humble yourself and take it, or maintain your pride and stay."

"Sarah, I cannot make this decision," Micah begged.

"But you must," his sister interjected. "Whatever decision you make, I promise I will support you."

"Sarah-," Micah began, but she raised a hand to stop him.

"Take care to make the right decision Micah, whatever that may be," and with her final word spoken, she left him. Micah watched her retreat down the little trail and gradually disappear. The herd did not move for some time, and as the sun fell they nestled into the grass. Micah sat on the saddle of the tree; his shoulders sagged and his heels dug into the dirt. Not for a single moment could he tear his eyes from the horizon.

DEFERENCE

Those driven by the insatiable pursuit are a minority by the hand of time alone. As the pendulum swings, their number decays. Only the foolish liken themselves to stone, for it is in the nature of man to be malleable. Though one can never truly forget that which held his heart captive, he can dull its memory. To surrender to that first love is to accept a life of pain. Time is an enduring form of torture, and under its influence the majority succumbs to more honorable pursuits.

The moon had long since risen by the time Micah latched the herd into their wooden pen for the night. After a cursory inspection of the lock, he rested his aching head on the gate. The day had taxed him emotionally and he was no closer to a decision than when his sister had left him. Contradictory feelings still rumbled from deep within his chest but his tired conscience could hardly discern between them anymore.

The evening air blew softly, tickling the grass and whistling around the cabin walls. The fields maintained a choked silence; even the herd had retired without a sound to the pen. Micah made no effort to combat the stillness. He allowed it to permeate his consciousness. He invited the empty as a welcomed guest, excusing the former occupants of his mind without hesitation. One by one they shuffled out, shouting and arguing as they had for hours prior. But the void did not speak, for it did not need to. It simply stood and observed from a vantage of shadow.

Micah enjoyed the quiet for some time, but slowly grew aware of his guest's unrelenting stare. The emptiness drew closer to Micah, and he saw expectation burn in its abysmal eyes. And as the empty approached it slipped out of the darkness. Micah watched in horror as the eyes quivered and shook with guilt: a guilt he recognized as his own. In a flash the empty rushed upon Micah, forcing a dark blade into his stomach and injecting him with the guilt he had avoided for so long. With a gasp Micah fell to his knees. He cradled his head in his hands and twisted his hair between his fingers.

A light creaking of wooden hinges rode the wind over to Micah's crumpled figure. Startled, he regained his footing and turned to face the source. The door to his home stood open wide, and his father stood beside it, illuminated by the flicker of the hearth inside. His father said nothing but gently closed the door before picking his way through the grass to Micah.

"Father, why are you out so late?" Micah implored, trying to direct the conversation from his compromised position. His father made no reply but instead steadied himself on the wooden railing. His father no longer resembled the tall, cutting figure of Micah's childhood. He supported a broken frame with a knobby cane; his back was bent from many seasons of labor and his right knee was stiff from a lasting injury. Micah immediately bent to help his father regain balance.

"Thank you Micah," his father nodded. He placed a firm hand on the fence and assumed a square stance. "I can manage myself now." A smile lurked behind a gray bushel of hair, but his eyes searched Micah's face in earnest. "Have you had any trouble with the herd? As you say, the hour is late."

"No trouble, we simply wandered too far," Micah said reassuringly. His father nodded in return.

"Sometimes it is easy to lose the trail. But you always find yourself home." Micah's father shifted on his feet. "I know that Sarah spoke to you today." Micah's face lit up in surprise, but his father interjected quickly, "She didn't tell me what you spoke of, only that you were distressed. Your mother and I have noticed it as well. Micah, is there something you need to tell me?"

Micah watched the moonlit fields ripple and flash. "No Father. Sarah must be mistaken; I was not distressed."

His father continued to watch him carefully. "And your mother and I, we too were mistaken?" Micah did not answer, but instead turned his attention to the soil around his feet. His eyes were distant, and his lips were drawn tight. Micah's father acknowledged his response without a word, and took a moment to compose himself. "I told you when you were young of how I came to our home, have I not?"

"You have."

"But you must have then only aged a handful of seasons. No, I did not tell you all. What you do not know is that I did not simply come to this valley for fortune's sake. From beyond the watershed we were all told stories of the fertility of these fields. They filled my young mind with hope; for an entire season my mind ran away with ideas and prospects. It was enough to drive me mad!

"My father was a blacksmith. He did well for himself, and had respect for tradition, as it had won him a considerable status in our village. He wished for me to take up the hammer as he had for his father. I did this for some time. But while my body worked in his smithy, my mind fled to the fields of the valley. It didn't take much time to pass before my father observed this quality in me.

"This infuriated him. His rage burned hotter than the furnace, and he took to punishing me for my treason. Your grandfather was not a wicked man, Micah. But his 'corrections' forced my mind always further from the anvil. And I did not require much convincing; as soon as I had a sufficient sum to my name I left my father. My journey ended at our home, much as it is today."

At this Micah's father paused. Micah, feeling exposed, did not venture to speak. His father stroked his chin thoughtfully before resuming. "Do not be so concerned, for I have no intention of acting as my father had towards me. He was misguided, he did not understand youth. Micah, I have lived many seasons, and I have felt as you do now. But hear me well, my decision was a mistake that I regret deeply.

"I broke our family that day. I have never returned, and I would not be welcomed if I were to. And at what price? The herd is growing Micah, but it has taken my entire life to yield what little we have. Your grandfather worked his hands raw so that I would be comfortable, so that I might work less. And I insulted him Micah, I insulted him far deeper than I ever intended, for I did not understand his sacrifice."

Micah's father fixed his eyes on him. "Do not do something that you will regret my son. Time will heal your suffering, if only you allow it."

"Yes father." Micah's face burned with shame. He did not dare face his father who had since removed his withering stare. They stood side by side at the rail. The evening wind had been reduced to a delicate breeze that broke like water over Micah's emblazoned cheeks. His father split the silence with a haggard cough.

"You should get some rest. Come inside, the air is getting cold." His father clapped a calloused hand on Micah's back for support and took a tentative step towards the door.

"Yes, I am very tired," Micah admitted. And together they entered their home.

That evening promised little sleep for Micah. As the moon gently rolled across the sky, Micah lay awake on his bedspread. His body begged for sleep, but his eyes obeyed the protest of his conscience. The guilt that had struck him continued to froth and boil from the depths of his stomach. In the falling hours of the night, the cold had begun to constrict the cabin walls. Micah listened to them creak and groan as they shifted under the encroaching freeze. Although he could not distinguish the walls of his chamber in the darkness, he felt as though they had been reduced to the size of a coffin. Should he simply extend a hand before his face, he felt certain that it would encounter the confines of his cell. The effect was toxic, claustrophobic, and nausea accompanied his already stricken state. After a considerable effort to endure the conditions, Micah decided that it was intolerable. He rose from his bed, and stumbled to dress himself. Aware of the chill that awaited him, he bundled himself tightly in his warmest attire. As an afterthought, Micah grabbed his goatskin rucksack and tossed several sheets inside, motivated by the notion of not spending another minute of the night in his strangling chamber. Satisfied, Micah crept through the main room of his home and stepped out once again into the outside air.

DECISION

Commitment to the first love requires more than fortitude of mind. Should reason and logic dangle without foundation, they may be construed into choice's greatest enemy. For those who are lost, the decision is no longer a task of reason, but is motivated by the soul. Fate bends her knees to listen, the soul conspires with the cosmos, and the choice will be made for the chooser.

The road was straight and narrow. Tall stalks of grass ran on either side as far as the eye could see. The road ran north. Its terminus was the horizon, interrupted by the jagged palisade of The Divide. The peaks glowed white, reflecting the eminent light of the heavens above. Despite the season, snow and ice still clung desperately to its purchase. It rallied in anticipation of the coming dawn.

Micah walked with his eyes locked on the horizon. From the moment he stepped outside the cabin, The Divide absorbed his attention. He walked north, without intention, simply drawn to that which summoned him. But gradually his curiosity was overcome with a familiar cold.

He felt his old fears flash and threaten his pace. His muscles tightened, his step became stiff, and he came to a gradual halt. Micah became rooted to the earth. The Divide taunted him. It dominated his vision; it enveloped his mind and gripped his heart. The mountains swam before him, and his head began to spin and turn in unison. Suddenly, his feet were released, and Micah took a step backwards to regain his balance. He shook himself, and reacquired the horizon. Micah blinked, taken aback by what he now beheld.

A brilliant canvas of light sprouted out from behind the Northern Divide and rolled itself out and across the night sky. It stretched overhead in a spectacular arc, falling behind the southern horizon. It was composed of uncountable stars, each so precisely distinct and yet simultaneously blurred into the single stroke of a celestial paintbrush, drawn along the underside of an infinite dome of darkness.

As Micah craned his neck further to take in the expanse, its dark, glittering ceiling seemed to translate further into the void. The deeper he stared, the further it slipped away. An irrational fear perturbed him, and he madly tried to focus on a single star to prevent its escape. But the sky seemed to accelerate its depth in response, confounding any sense of scale. Soon it too escaped into the infinite.

A light tingling swept over Micah. He watched the cosmic roof hang indifferently above him. Lost among its contents, he was a child again, incapable of understanding the reality he perceived. And as this sensation developed in him, he was overcome with sincere humility. The realm of the gods glittered so distinctly, observable even to his mortal eye, and yet was hopelessly beyond his comprehension.

The Divide, previously so daunting in magnitude, was dwarfed in comparison to the cosmic ceiling above. Its peaks stretched hungrily towards the heavens, but fell impossibly short of the infinity they desired. Micah felt a sense of unity with their endeavor as he stood beside and gazed into heaven.

"Even The Divide wants to be greater," Micah wondered aloud. The words escaped his lips inadvertently, and surprised him in doing so. And at their conception, Micah felt an old ember flicker and catch fire in his chest. The guilt that had swollen in his body began to deflate; it blew through his chest and fueled the flame that burned there.

Micah squared his shoulders to the horizon once more, and began to walk.

He could hear his heart pounding in his ears. With every step he forgot himself. His body trembled and burned, the fire pulsated through his veins. Even his father's words, still echoing in his mind, were soon devoured by the hungry blaze. He was reduced to animalistic intention, a pure desire: insatiable, unflinching, and unafraid. He required no further justification, for The Divide had provided it for him. And his soul, so starved and so bitterly hungry, lurched at the opportunity without reserve. His mind pulled at the reigns at first, but eventually acquiesced.

Reality had loosened its hold on Micah, and he did not notice the tavern come and go as he marched down the road. But his presence did not go unnoticed. For Edgar had spent the evening trying to find the bottom of a bottomless tap, and had been forcibly removed from the tavern due to riotous behavior. Unfortunately for Edgar he was intensely afraid of returning home to his wife in an inebriated state, so he had relinquished the remainder of his evening to sobering himself under the night sky.

Edgar sat on the steps leading to the tavern porch in a state of thick boredom, sneaking wistful glances through the front door and humming along with the players inside, when Micah strode out before him. Micah wore a determined expression, and he made no gesture or acknowledgement as he passed. Amused and grateful for the distraction, Edgar sprung from the steps and hailed Micah.

"Slow down there, what's got you in a hurry?" Micah did not break stride. This further delighted Edgar. "Hello there Micah, where are you off to?" he tried louder.

Micah twitched, the spell was broken, and his feet ground to a halt. He turned, and searched for his caller. Edgar struggled to catch up with him, waddling from his nocturnal endeavors.

"Edgar?" Micah inquired, squinting in the dark.

"Yes Micah!" Edgar confirmed happily. "You are not enjoying the evening as you should be my friend- it is best spent with company!" For emphasis, he clapped Micah on the arm in what he believed to be a friendly fashion; however, to Micah felt more akin to a blow.

"Not tonight," Micah stammered. He made a slight movement away from Edgar, which the latter anticipated by swooping in closer still.

Edgar grabbed Micah by the arm and turned towards the tavern, pointing. "The lute players are here tonight; can you hear the music? It is very beautiful; you really should not miss it!"

"It is very beautiful Edgar; I can hear it." Micah glanced desperately over his shoulder. "Why don't you go back inside and enjoy it?"

Edgar opened his mouth to answer, but then thought better of it. "I'll be honest with you Micah, because you are a friend. The damned bartender has turned me out, and won't listen to reason. Perhaps I had lost my manners, I am a humble man and admit my faults. But now I have gathered myself and am absolutely amiable! I implore you, you must help me plead my case! You are known to be a reasonable man; the keeper will certainly listen to you!"

"Edgar, I cannot help you, I'm sorry. I am, occupied," Micah finished lamely, shrugging.

"I am sad to hear it Micah! Is it really so important that you cannot help a friend in desperate need? Why, what will the gods say when you ask for their blessing? They will tell you, those who do not bless do not deserve blessing!"

"Then I bless you Edgar, and wish you all the luck in gaining entry."

"That is very cruel indeed!" exclaimed Edgar, incredulous. "You make a mockery of my tribulation, and I find offense in that," he fumed. But it seemed that his fuse ran short, for soon he adopted an inquisitive look. "Micah, now is a very strange time for walking. Are you up to mischief tonight? I may be compelled to report such conduct to your father."

"That is not necessary," Micah replied quickly. "I simply desired the fresh air, and needed to stretch my legs."

Edgar shook his head. "Your 'pleasure walk' is very determined then. No, I think you are lying to me. Don't think you can pull the bag over my eyes, even in this state. Be honest with me Micah, or your father will hear of it!"

"Edgar, there is no reason for your questions, and no need to bring my family into this!"

"That's it," Edgar said, raising a finger. "On my honor your father will be told!"

"Then let it be, it makes no difference!" Micah snapped. Edgar involuntarily jerked back at the sudden outburst. He still held his index finger pointedly, but it swayed in the evening breeze. He appeared deflated, as if a strong wind had just expired in his sails. Micah made no effort to occupy the silence that ensued.

"But Micah, you really should care, he is your father after all," Edgar very nearly begged.

"I do care Edgar, but my father will know by your mouth or by another." He let out a deep sigh. "And why should it not be from yours? At least I can dictate your message and not sacrifice myself to rumor. Edgar, my friend, I will not be seeing you or anyone else for some time. I'm afraid I will be leaving, tonight."

"Leaving? To where?" Edgar wore an incredulous expression.

"To the City of the Gods, Edgar. I have tried to convince myself otherwise, I have tried to find my place in the fields, but I cannot ignore the calling of my soul. I feel myself drawn beyond The Divide, like slipping down a muddy hillside. As much as it terrifies me, as much as I ignore its call, I know in my heart and my mind that I will succumb. It is as you see me tonight, defeated, moving like a lamb to the slaughter. But I find no respite in the ignorance of a lamb, for I am aware of the nature of my decision.

"Tell my father that I have listened and understood his warning. Tell him that I recognize the risk I am about to take. And be sure that he understands that I am well convinced of my own inevitable failure. But, also remind him of the hope he felt as a youth, remind him of how the fields settled so deeply in his heart and of how they wrestled his will and sense from him. I do not ask him to forgive me for I do not expect his forgiveness, but I do wish for him to try to understand my decision."

While Micah spoke Edgar's look of incredulity bloomed into disbelief. He tried to interrupt several times, but was flatly ignored. When Micah finished Edgar waited for an exaggerated moment to ensure his orator was indeed at a close, at which he very loudly established his opinion.

"This is foolish indeed! To the City of the Gods, Micah? Over The Divide? My friend, what makes you think that if you can cross The Divide, you will find the City? You even doubt yourself of your decision, and rightfully so! It is absolutely destined to fail! You will gain nothing; you have not a single chance of hope!" Edgar ran out of breath while speaking and so stopped to gather himself.

"I stand to gain everything Edgar," Micah whispered. "Should I succeed, I will have become more than myself. If I stay, I gain nothing. I will forever be the man you see before you. And that terrifies me more than The Divide, and more than the shame I will bear."

"You are mistaken, you are young and are carried away by radical notions!"

"Yes," Micah admitted. "I am carried away. Is it strange that I know so, and yet choose to follow? I suppose it is strange." His eyes were lost to the horizon.

"Strange? It is not only strange but idiotic!" Edgar's finger decidedly leapt forward once again. His words however fell on deaf ears. Micah had receded once more into his mind, and could no longer be coaxed out with accusations. Edgar, noticing this, resigned himself to a less aggressive approach. "Micah my friend, a good man does not make such base decisions! Now please rid yourself of these vile thoughts, join me in the tavern and let us celebrate your maturity with ale, music and company. And what company; all the women of the valley must be in this very tavern tonight, I swear it by the gods! Come now, what do you say to that?" A lecherous grin crawled across his countenance.

Micah did not answer immediately. Edgar's voice echoed from a hollow, far-away place. "No. My mind is set; I will not go back. Goodbye; I hope that someday I will return." And without so much as a parting glance, Micah walked north.

For a long time, Edgar watched Micah walk the straight and narrow road. When his friend was finally taken by the shadows, Edgar managed to break himself from his watch. "Well," he muttered to himself, "I wager that was sobering enough," and trudged up the steps to the tavern door.

II. the Divide

DESIRE

When a seeker becomes devoted to their soul, they are introduced to an aspect of themselves previously imprisoned by lock and key. This new form of self is spirited, reckless, and wonderful. It imbues even the most wretched qualities of life with meaning, and the sensation is as fantastic as it is addictive.

An azure sky stretched over rolling hills of stone. The sun hovered unshrouded by clouds, the rock below greedily consuming its heat. Few trees ventured to sprout from the weaknesses in the stone cap, and offered little shelter. The terrain ran wet with snowmelt, eager to be reclaimed by the warmth of the sun. It gurgled along channels carved by the passage of time.

The valley below shimmered and swam with its usual afternoon wind. From the vantage of the hills, Micah could survey the entire world that encompassed his youth. He sat cross-legged on bare stone, squinting against the high noon sun. He reached a hand forward, and closing one eye watched with amazement as his open palm easily erased that world from the landscape. A smile tickled across his face, and a great feeling of elation bubbled up from his chest.

Micah sprang to his feet, and threaded his arms through the straps of his rucksack. He regained his footsteps on the poorly marked trail he had been following for the day. It lacked any formal definition, but despite losing the main trail on multiple occasions he had found that all deviations eventually recovered the primary. The trail itself was steep, rugged and unlike anything Micah had experience in the valley. His calves burned, and his feet bruised over the unrelenting stone. He was forced to travel quite slowly.

But though the conditions only grew more demanding, Micah found his mood wholly exorbitant, almost drunk on the experience. As he passed ever higher into the foothills, his creaking body could not so much as perturb the power of his will. Though every footstep was accompanied with pain and protest, his form bent easily under sheer subconscious force of mind. Micah thought very little as he climbed. His mind swam only with intention and desire.

The sun marched steadily across the sky, and soon the light threatened to hide beyond the crest of rock above. Micah, noticing this, quickened his pace and began to take note of potential campsites. His breath grew short, and he found himself gasping desperately for air. He stopped beside a lip of rock, and placed a hand on it for support. Before long Micah could subsist on long draws from his nose, and in doing so noticed a familiar smell. Noting that his surroundings were incongruous with the scent, he pulled himself beyond the rib of stone and peered up the hillside.

In the distance, about a thousand paces from his position, dark smoke could be seen curling into the sky above. The breeze stole the smoke and passed it along to Micah, who had immediately guessed its purpose. His stomach rumbled, and Micah set off in haste to make himself known, hoping to secure a place beside the fire and perhaps to share in a meal. It had been some time since Micah had been in company; the roads of The Divide were seldom traveled.

As Micah drew closer he could distinguish not several but many voices amidst a din and clatter of livestock and machinery. Surmounting a final ridge crest, Micah found himself staring across a sparkling mountain lake nestled within the shoulders of two massive, polished rock domes. To his great surprise, a bustling village sprouted amongst a wooded grove that ran along the opposite shore. He could see men, women, and children walking about what appeared to be a modest market, trading goods such as linens, livestock and various trinkets. At the center of the village a great fire was maintained over which Micah could see a spitted pig roasting. He found it difficult to maintain focus on anything but the pig, and started to pick his way through the rocks along the lakeshore.

"Now stranger," a voice burst out from over Micah's right shoulder, "Don't be in such a hurry, I would much like to make your acquaintance."

40

Startled, Micah turned to identify the voice. It belonged to a young man, perhaps of his same age, dressed in rugged attire. He sat amongst the large boulders that were grouped by the lake. He wore no shoes, and a flimsy wooden rod was placed across his lap. He appeared to be in the process of baiting a line before Micah had unwittingly walked by his position.

"I'm sorry sir, I did not see you." Micah apologized.

"No, but it is perhaps my fault, I have not made my position easily known." He grinned, revealing a set of crooked teeth. "Where have you come from? Please, sit, I know it may not be as agreeable as the fire," he nodded at the village, "But I do have some morsels to share if you will grant me your story." With a welcoming smile, the man opened a dirty rag and revealed a prior catch that had already been treated with flame. Micah wrenched his eyes from the fire and took a seat by the villager.

"Of course, I would be happy to, though my story is not much to share I'm afraid."

"I've heard many stories, and am always happy to hear another. You come from the valley?"

"Yes."

"And where are you headed? Surely ours is not your destination," he smiled again.

"Well no, I'm afraid I've found yours quite by accident. I am traveling across The Divide, to the City of the Gods."

"Ah," the villager acknowledged knowingly. "It is not unique you know; we encounter many with such intentions. But to conquer The Divide, it is a noble goal indeed! Are you, a man of the valley, certain that you can rise to its heights? Why, have you any knowledge of The Divide?"

Micah frowned, "No sir, I have never been outside the cradle of the valley. I feel as though I am a baby fresh from the womb, but there is a spirit inside me that has awakened among the rock. As you suggest, I am not certain I can rise to such great heights. But as you see before you, with every step that I take I am higher than ever before. My spirit is hungry, insatiable, and I am powerless to stop it."

41

The man laughed. "I know your type well. You are of the right breed, my new friend, to be among the great hills. You are in good company now, for the men of the valley cannot understand men such as ourselves. We live here at the very doorstep of The Divide. Every bitter storm, every winter, we endure and we overcome." He stuck his chest vigorously. "The Twisted Peak rises above, and we are its people. And friend, I believe you are the same."

The villager's eyes left Micah, and wandered into the deep sky above. Micah followed his gaze. Towering above the village, beyond the rolling hills of stone, protruded the pale wall of The Divide, closer now than ever before. And from its flanks a black summit was rooted. It broke hungrily away from its siblings, clamoring for heaven on the backs of their lesser remains. And in a final, greedy attempt for glory, the mountain twisted and strained its scarred summit against the shackles of earth. Micah had seen its terrible figure before.

"It is good to meet those who are likeminded," Micah returned his attention to his company. "I would be quite grateful for your wisdom as a man who has lived in this fearsome land."

"And I would be delighted to help a friend," the man bowed. "Come now, the fish are not biting this evening, let us enjoy the fire together." They stood, and Micah helped him collect his belongings before starting for the village. As they walked they spoke of life in the foothills, of the bitter winters and of life in the valley. They talked of the travelers who passed through the village and of the wondrous stories they had shared. Upon reaching the village, they were warmly welcomed by its inhabitants, and Micah was ushered to the fireplace. He was offered a choice cut of meat and a cup of mountain spirit. He found the drink quite potent, and soon drifted into an agreeable mood alongside his gracious hosts.

As evening fell, the village gathered by the fire for warmth. Some danced, others sang, and most simply watched the flame flicker and spark. Micah and his new companion sat removed from the general population. They faced north, and contemplated the dark figures that dominated the skyline.

"Zachary, you have seen many travel through your village—I wonder if you recount a particular man by the name of Giralt?" Micah trained a curious eye on his neighbor.

Zachary pondered for a moment. "I recall such a man. Not an easy one to forget. He did not stay long, but the impression he left has yet to clear our minds. Odd man, but one of the few to surmount the Twisted Peak. He made well sure that all of us would remember it."

"Truly, he has done as he says?" Micah gasped in astonishment.

Zachary shrugged in return. "He was seen climbing high on its southwest shoulder. And in two days following, he paraded through our town carrying the black rock of the summit. I cannot doubt my eyes, though I might doubt his character."

"The Twisted Peak," Micah chewed his words thoughtfully, "It is the highest summit of The Divide?"

The light of the fire flashed across his countenance. His eyes glowed, and even after the fire had subsided maintained a vestige of that aura. Zachary paused to choose his words. "Micah, I have heard many stories of The Divide, I have heard of no summit more malevolent than our own. It is a cruel peak, and men more travelled than yourself frequently perish on its slopes."

"Have you ever attempted the summit?"

"You must understand; our people battle through the seasons alongside the Twisted Peak. We feel the same thunder of the heavens; it is the justice of the gods to punish those who covet such great heights."

"Have you attempted any summit, Zachary?" Micah's words were delivered as bluntly as a hammer, utterly devoid of reservation.

"Well, no I have not done so myself," replied Zachary, obviously hurt. He furrowed his brow, and paused to contemplate his damaged position. "Our village is a refuge to such men, and though I hold in high esteem those who strive for such honor, I have duties to attend. Why, if it were not for men such as myself, men such as you would find no respite from the horrors of The Divide. It is no slight task; it is a constant battle for survival. Traders, travelers, and dreamers alike need my village's support! You see Micah, your question is damning by nature. I can see that you believe your task is noblest of all, but you forget that the noble man cannot succeed on skill and fortune alone. And so I ask, what is nobler? The man who strives for a great honor, or the man who sacrifices his own life to enable another?"

His words cut Micah like a blade. The wound bled green with guilt, and a small voice resurfaced from the depths of his subconscious. It cried out in pain.

"My new friend, I have ungraciously challenged your very purpose, I am deeply sorry for it. Please forgive me; I'm afraid I have become quite taken with my own intentions and it has moved me to improper conclusions." Micah's voice cracked with emotion. His eyes dimmed, and his cheeks flushed with hot shame.

"There is no need to apologize," Zachary insisted. "My people are hard; words alone cannot shake my foundation. I prefer you tend to honesty; it is an admirable quality. But if you pose an honest question, expect honesty in reply.

"For the sake of truthfulness, I must admit that I too have felt the summons of the Twisted Peak. And how could I not? Every day I have walked under its shadow, but as it requires no repeating, my place is with my people, and I cannot let my mind wander up such a great slope." Zachary finished with a little shrug.

"Is it wrong to subdue your desire?" Micah wondered aloud.

"It is reckless to unleash it. My friend, if by some miracle you did summit the Twisted Peak, what then would you do?"

Though he did not admit it, Micah had not considered anything further than the summit. He became alarmingly aware of his own myopia, but for fear of revealing his naivety struggled to conjure some reason for his desire. "Why, I would use the vantage to survey The Divide. It is my intention to cross, I seek the City after all."

Zachary shook his head and frowned. "I know of the most direct route through the mountains, The Divide has a weakness over Three Finger Pass, just beyond the Cleaver on

44

the western slopes of the Twisted Peak. To gain a summit would not only be dangerous, but an unnecessary waste of resources. No my friend, I cannot advise that you pursue any other avenue. Look now, as the spring brings the thaw the gods awaken to punish those still reaching for the sky!"

He raised a gloved finger and directed Micah's attention north, but the gesture was unnecessary as a deep and resonant rumble shook the village by its very foundations, drawing Micah to it. Dark clouds blotted out the stars above; they spiraled tightly around the black summit of The Divide and threatened to engulf its thorny crown. But the Twisted Peak did not cower. It bore its battle-scarred face to heaven and was delivered a mighty retribution. From beyond the curtain of cloud the gods unleashed their jealousy and hatred upon the wretched challenger. Brilliant streaks of blue and white broke over its formidable head, accompanied by the booming roars of the gods that released them. The summit became holy death by which even stone shook and cracked. And though its brow splintered, still the Twisted Peak did not tremble. The clouds circled above impatiently, and at the word of their masters descended, devouring its stubborn crest. The tall shoulders of The Divide rose into the cloud, a writhing, incoherent mass of blinding light and impenetrable darkness under which the Twisted Peak alone endured its tribulation.

"What must it be like Zachary, to be among the gods?" Micah breathed as he watched the great forces of heaven and earth collided above. His companion watched him closely.

"Even the Twisted Peak cannot reach heaven." A spectacular blue arc illuminated the stone hills surrounding them, causing Zachary to falter and look north. "The old ones tell us the stories of the mountains. Our peak is young, and eager. But time will bend its knee. The lesser peaks, they are old, they have been blackened and punished by the gods in their own time. See how they hide now beneath the clouds? They fear judgement. As we all should, Micah."

"My friend," Micah smiled, drawn from his fixed stare, "You are beyond your age. I hope that in my coming travels, I gain but half of your wisdom."

"Heed these warnings, and you will have had all of it."

45

Together they watched The Divide until the fire had burned to an ember. The air grew cold, and shivering in the evening air Zachary led Micah to his home for the night. His host provided him with substantial accommodations, but still Micah did not sleep well. Visions of The Divide and its black tower had burned into his subconscious.

LUST

The curious few are no more; hunger blossoms into gluttony. The object of love becomes a platter with which to satiate the insatiable. And like a hound, the seeker sees nothing but the fabulous feast, drooling for promised reward. But the hound must earn every meal. And the larger the game, the more fearsome the pursuit.

The following morning sung with activity; red jays squabbled in the boughs of the little grove and early risers prepared for their daily work. What villagers had gathered in the streets bid Micah farewell, as he had resolved to make for the Three Finger Pass in light of favorable conditions. The sky was clear but for a light haze, and the wind hummed softly along the foothills.

Zachary insisted upon accompanying Micah to the foot of The Divide, where he could best indicate the route forward. Together they passed through the village glades and stepped foot upon the stone hills. The trail was faint, marked indiscriminately with little pillars of rock. Micah was grateful for the company; his host knew the path well.

The trail snaked its way around glittering lakes, through disjoint patches of scrubby foliage, and through tight weaknesses in The Divide's humblest perimeter walls. It never took the direct or obvious route, but instead seemed to pleasure itself in confounding travelers with an apparently roundabout or backpedaling trail that always managed to mysteriously deliver the destination. And it did not descend, but continued to rise above the valley below, now lost in dreary haze that collected low on the rocks.

Their conversation helped to pass the time; Zachary was keen to share his knowledge and Micah absorbed it readily. Zachary made a worthy effort to identify unique plants and creatures, as well as potential dangers that lay in wait deep within the mountains. He spoke quickly, and paused only to confirm that each point was received. Micah easily surrendered to the arrangement. The incline continued to steepen, and every breath was laborious under Zachary's fast pace. But Zachary seemed not to notice; as they drew ever closer to the great white wall he became increasingly desperate to imbue Micah with practical wisdoms.

The sun had crawled far across the sky, and began to slip behind the spine of The Divide. The trail had deposited Zachary and Micah into a vast open space, a desert of stone and earth that was violently interrupted by the feet of the great white wall itself. Now directly above rose the Twisted Peak, a scar upon a shield of sparkling stone. Black gendarmes sprouted like fingers from its shoulders and the sun flitted between them, casting long shadows that crawled over the trail below.

"See where the sun rests? That is the Three Finger Pass."

The sun bloomed through a triad of pillars located on a high saddle of the connecting ridge between the Twisted Peak and its westerly neighbor. It soared high above the plateau, faint in the lingering haze.

"You can follow the trail over the pass, and if you move quickly you might make camp below the saddle. And if you are caught high during a storm, do not tempt the gods, but gain cover."

They stopped beside a large stone pile that indicated the terminus of the foothills and the doorstep of The Divide. The path, already faint, vanished beyond the marker. Here Zachary turned to face Micah. His face was stretched into a grim smile, but his eyes flashed with energy.

"Friend, a great adventure awaits you. Perhaps someday I will hear of it. Few are those who cross The Divide, and word travels well among them."

Micah returned his smile in earnest. "Zachary, you have been far too kind to one so undeserving! Maybe I am forgetting myself again; I believe that it is not I, but you who should claim such an opportunity. Even now I see it in your eyes! Don't you wish to see what it is you have heard so much about? Don't you want to feel the earth move under your feet, to find your place among the clouds? How can you stand there with the knowledge that every step forward is further than the last?"

Micah's emotion had leapt forward unrestrained, and left him breathless. A coal sputtered and caught fire from the depths of Zachary's untrained eyes. It held but for a moment, for Zachary's breath tightened and the little flame was quietly suffocated, leaving nothing but a puff of smoke that clouded his gaze.

"It is not my place." The words came slowly. "Please, do not take advantage of me now, here where I am at my weakest."

"My friend, if it is in your heart to do so-," Micah pleaded.

"I am no slave to my heart!"

Zachary's face was no longer warm, but was instead drawn into a viscous snarl. Micah bit back a response, and took pause to recover himself. Zachary did the same; his fierce expression peeled away leaving only lines of remorse.

"You should be leaving now Micah, the road is long and the day is short." Zachary's voice was low, reserved. He watched Micah from the corner of his eye.

"I will not leave you like this Zachary, I did not wish for there to be hard feelings between us. I value your friendship." Micah faltered. "I spoke from a place of fear; I realize that now. The road is lonely, and I was afraid to go alone."

Zachary grunted, and waved a forgiving hand. "There will be no hard feelings between us friend. I know that you are well-intentioned. I am a fool for forgetting it." His voice softened, and with a grin he took Micah by the hand. "Take care of yourself, and remember that fear may be your greatest ally in these mountains."

They embraced briefly, and then with a few parting words Zachary turned back down the long road to his home. Micah faced The Divide alone. A bitter cold occupied the place that Zachary once stood. Forcing solitude from his mind, Micah sized up the task before him. The pass was perched impossibly high above. Below the pass the great wall of The Divide seem to fracture and crumble, leaving a ruinous ramp to its weakness. Shouldering his pack, Micah started forward.

When Micah gained the ramp he found that it was composed entirely of large, loose boulders. Near the base the boulders were as large as small cottages, and Micah was forced to circumnavigate each, which greatly slowed his pace. And with every step, the incline grew. Micah's lungs quickly became grateful for the careful pace, though his heart still burned for the saddle above.

As Micah climbed higher and higher, the boulders shrank to stones, and soon he slipped and slid over a loose talus slope. Every step gained sank half a step into the crumbling earth. He frequently lost his footing and could only arrest a fall by sinking fingers deep into the rocks before him. Micah searched madly for some remnant of a trail; he feared that in his haste he had missed a critical landmark. But the ramp was blank save for the rubble that clung to its surface. So Micah continued his battle directly.

In his frenzy to achieve the pass, he took no note of elevation or time as he climbed. Although his body was damp with sweat, his face was dry and numb due to a prevailing wind. His fingers carried no life but felt as bone wrapped by a canvas of skin, claws intended not for warmth but for clinging. His legs bore a dull pain with every step, and his lips were sticky and cold.

His world was dark, his body shivered, but inside Micah blazed with hot fire. It consumed him, greedy for nourishment. He gasped and wheezed to stoke the flame. In return it burned away his pain, and cranked his legs endlessly. His figure became a chain upon which he choked himself, desperate for the pass above. And like an animal he climbed.

The sun set, and The Divide was enveloped in darkness. Micah could not see save for ten paces above and below himself; the guiding light of heaven was hidden above a thin shield of cloud. So he climbed until the slope gave out, rolling off into a sharp lip of rock. As the grade lightened, his fire died, and a veil of smoke lifted from his mind. Micah grew aware of his surroundings, and resolved to make camp wherever possible. Stumbling blindly in the dark, he found a soft patch of earth nestled underneath a stone wedge. By stretching his tarpaulin over the entrance, he was able to

50

significantly cut off the wind. Fighting off fatigue that set deep into his joints, Micah dug out his warmest clothes and blankets from his pack. He wrapped himself tightly within his sheets and before his head touched the earth descended into a fitful sleep.

EUPHORIA

To the wretch starved of all that is wholesome and delicious, the feast is an insurmountable temptation. The beggar does not fast, nor is he praised for a resiliency to the wiles of gluttony. The beggar is a slave because he is deprived. The beggar eats when he is able. And if the beggar is able to indulge, he will not resist any facet of that indulgence.

Soft light glowed through the tarpaulin. It warmed the rock and fought back the crisp mountain air. Micah let a long, foggy breath escape his lips, and his eyes cracked open. Tearing the tarpaulin away, he stepped out of his shelter and took in the world with bleary astonishment. He stood upon a narrow catwalk of rock, thrust vertically into an imposing atmosphere of thick gray. His perch was lost in fog through which the morning light weakly permeated, dense and damp to his naked skin. Before him the stone rampart crumbled and rolled downwards into the mist. Behind him the rock ended abruptly in a vertical cliff below which no bottom could be seen.

The catwalk ran east to west along the fortress wall of The Divide. It rose out of the clouds to the east and climbed steadily west, a shackle upon the western shoulder of the Twisted Peak. Its kin pulled tightly at the chain, and the rib was stretched thin.

Micah gathered his belongings. To his dismay the morning light had not brought any evidence of a trail, and the fog constrained his view to immediate surroundings. He peered into the gloomy depths north of the great white wall, squinting for any glimmer of a descent route but could find none. Uncertain, Micah gripped his pack straps tightly and began to wander east. The grade was shallow, and travel was easy.

The cloud befuddled all senses of time and scale. The world of gray earth and of gray air he had infiltrated was stifling and cold; he felt the mountains were wholly indifferent to his insignificant form. His feet left no prints on the stone, and his sound was devoured quickly into the thick atmosphere. Micah kicked loose rocks into the void beyond the wall just to hear the earth acknowledge his presence with the periodic clatter of stone upon stone.

He had not traveled far when a dark figure loomed out of the mist above him. A vast finger of rock curled over the southern edge of the wall. As Micah kept walking, two more fingers joined the first. His heart leapt as he recognized the gendarmes of the Three Finger Pass. Between the index and forefinger, a rough cairn was arranged, and crudely hewn steps worked their way down the southern slopes. Excited, Micah moved north and discovered that the cliff had receded into a sharp, rocky descent. An old handwoven rope, faded and frayed, served as a guideline down the terrible precipice. It was fastened to a forged eyebolt that had been hammered indelicately into an open crack in the stone many seasons ago.

After giving the rope a considerable test of weight, Micah was satisfied in its design. He was not without reservation stepping over the northern edge of The Divide, but it felt good to again have a sense of direction. But as Micah found purchase below the lip of the rampart, he chanced a final glance east, and froze. The little catwalk he had occupied wandered dreamily into the mist. And at the very edge of his vision a single stone lay alone on the gray rock of the pass. It was a black stone, dark as the behemoth it had departed long ago.

The air was still. Not a wisp of mountain wind swept the ridge. Micah held the black stone in his hands, and turned it over thoughtfully. Before his boots the rock buckled and turned black. A dark staircase of crumbling rock climbed drearily above. His ankles felt the tilt of the earth, and his legs coiled for the punishment of the slope. Micah's heart pounded. His body burned hot and cold alike, with fingers curled into needling tools and his chest a furnace driving the spokes of the machine. The black rock sucked warmth from his fingertips. It struck the ground with a clatter, setting in motion the wheels of Micah's will and flaring the canvas of his desire.

Micah's legs shot forward, struck like the unfettered locking of two rotating gears. The fire burned brightly, and hot smoke singed his flaring nostrils. His conscious mind shrank in fear from the creature that roared deep inside. It surrendered his faculties to that unshackled prisoner and sunk into the corner of his being. Micah's eyes saw only the next placement of a foot or hand, his mouth and nose gaped and drank deeply from the wet air, his ears turned inside out and heard nothing but the beating of his heart. He relished its song, it became the anthem of his suffering and the promise of his victory.

The ridge opened into the massive southwest shoulder of the Twisted Peak. Micah no longer walked a narrow path but instead crawled up a broken field of rock. The air grew colder as he climbed, and ice and snow ran down outcroppings like tears. The stone was loose, crumbling. He dug for holds, he kicked for steps. He carved a trench up the face of the mountain. His assault flung debris far out into open space, splattering their ruin over the very mountain from which they were born.

Black towers with rolling white eyes of snow and glittering fangs of ice lolled out of the mist. They bent their ugly skulls to heaven, each bitterly jealous of their higher neighbor. Some stretched their necks so thin that their bodies broke only to tumble to depths so far below. All whispered revenge as they slipped into the haze far below Micah's ascension.

The Twisted Peak never faltered in its defenses. It was shielded with sheer cliff faces, rivets of ice clogged with snow, and loose rock that threatened to send Micah hurtling into the abyss with one false move. But Micah's fury knew no limit. Without finesse, without thought, Micah broke through each obstacle. His animal eyes searched each and discovered the mountain's weakness without breaking stride. He did not stop, he lapped melt water as he moved along the stone and ate nothing. His head began to pound tremendously, but he gave it no regard. His hands ached from the cold but they received no care. As the peak twisted into the sky Micah followed, desperately coveting its blasphemous summit.

TERMINUS

There is no greater joy than the pursuit. The objective which sits so high, is so unattainable, is seen growing closer and closer still. Each step gained feeds the fire, each hungry glance rewarded with a new perspective of that mighty objective. The wretch below imagines himself upon that lonely point, an occupant of the heaven he so desires. An ideal, a vision of that perfect image they could never acquire. And yet as they move they feel its proximity. It warms them, it spurs them, and it shows them their own potential.

In a white flash Micah cut through the cloud and into the vast, open blue. The summit block stood above him, the proudest and most triumphant point of the Twisted Peak. It waited there alone, blackened and bent by the retribution of the gods. It stooped low, kneeling, broken. Weeping. Micah walked slowly to the withered block. He stepped easily upon its humbled frame. He stood atop the Twisted Peak.

The clouds stretched out to the horizon in all directions. And yet no longer were they a ceiling, but now a floor over which Micah stood. The dogs of heaven held no punishing hand over him; he was left not alone, but with the summit block atop that mound of jealous rocky flesh. And together they surveyed The Divide.

When Micah looked out he saw that even they were not truly alone. Hundreds of peaks pierced their brutish heads through the clouds. Some supported glittering helms of cold ice, others massive necks of earth, and few crowns of clean stone. He counted many that stood far higher than his own wilted summit which barely punctured the white valley. They towered mightily above the cloud, casting massive shadows across the valley of the gods without fear of tribulation.

Micah's flame washed out in a bitter flood. He was flattened; he struggled to draw breath and began to shake uncontrollably. He felt a deep stab of remorse and dismounted the lowly summit block of the Twisted Peak.

They shared the same modest height together. And together they sat and shed tears of shame at their meager accomplishment in the shadow of such great giants; the Twisted Peak tears of ice and snow and Micah of salt and water.

The sun travelled far across the sky during the time that the two shared the summit. Micah no longer wept, but simply watched as nightfall approached. His face was dry and blistering in the sun, but he did not care. He let the hot air lull his weary body into a stupor. His eyelids grew heavy, dropped, and he fell fast asleep.

REGRESSION

The moment the glutton, the brave traveler, the luster and the seeker, that very moment they reach terminus, they find not all is as desired from below. Terminus holds no reward, and promises nothing but retreat. The fool is led to some chosen end only to contemplate the abysmal return. And so all learn that the mountains are daunting to climb, but deadly to descend.

Micah woke with a shiver. The sun had dropped below the horizon, and with the falling temperature a high wind rose. He wrapped himself tightly in his goatskin coat and closed his eyes, begging to be drawn back into the silent world of sleep, to let his soul ride away along the slipstream of the wind, to be plucked mercifully from naked display, the tall mountains of The Divide laughing testaments to his worthlessness. He cradled his head in cold, pale fingers.

The night sky dominated the world above. It called softly, and yet so clearly as to cut like a blade through the howl of wind: the ring of a crystalline bell above crashing waves. Micah's ears were deaf to its whisper, but to his soul it beckoned. Micah lifted his face from his sheltering hands, and let his gaze swim into heaven above. The stars hung on their sparkling canvas, an infinity away. Micah lifted an open palm to heaven. The stars, his hands, he had seen them in contrast before. His fingers blocked no more of the night sky than they had in the valley. No closer than before, and further still. Nowhere to go, but down the mountain. To rest each foot comfortably in steps cut from his ascent when the sun still hung high, to place each step lower than the last. The notion curdled in his throat.

A faint rumble reverberated in the air like stones down a mountainside, stirring Micah. He needed no sound to guess its true source, for with it accompanied a malicious energy that crawled up his spine. Micah turned north, and what he beheld caused his body to tremble. The ocean of cloud once placid and white now frothed and swam, the Twisted Peak an island above a turbulent sea. And within the depths lurked the gods' manifestation of jealousy and rage, a demon of pure light. It rumbled and roared, striking each tall mountain at their feet, hungry to consume their proud bodies, desperate for the flesh who had coveted their summits. And with every strike it grew closer to the Twisted Peak.

Micah jumped to cower in the shelter of the summit block. But as he did a clap of light, wicked and tremendous, illuminated the wretched stone in a heart stopping flash. The Twisted Peak shed no more tears in the cold. Alone atop its unholy pedestal it curled in anxiety, in mortal terror, in abject fear of the retribution to come. It cradled its poor head, horribly beaten and scarred, and in the high wind released a piercing scream. It was the scream of the damned, the scream of one forsaken by the gods, of one who knew deeply the lashes of their hate. It howled at its chains and dreaded what was to and what always had come in the night.

The clouds rose like floodwater and the refuge of the mountain shrank. The beast now restlessly circled the Twisted Peak. In each flash its blinding form was burned into Micah's vision. Micah knelt at the summit, and hugged himself in terror. The Twisted Peak bore him to the sky, an offering so that the mountain might continue its climb. The clouds lapped at his feet, and he knew that his time was short. The inevitable fate that rose to consume him would have its victim.

On the horizon a black cloud surged, a tidal wave amidst the ocean. And the beast rode the wave, sparkling and flashing with malevolence. In the wind it soared high above the mountain, billowing with its awful presence. The summit block bowed before it and offered a final, ugly plea. But Micah turned from the summit, faced his route to ascension, and he ran down. The cloud washed over the summit, and he was lost to the dark sea.

Heaven offered no light through the thick darkness. Micah could see nothing; his world was small, confined, constricting: limited to the slap of loose rock beneath his feet and his own ragged breath. The slope steepened, and Micah moved too quickly to anticipate its changing. He slipped and fell, tumbling head over toe and arrested only by the accumulation of debris. For a moment he lay panting among the stone, dazed. He regained his footing tentatively. The wind abated, his feet were still, and he basked in an unearthly quiet. But a dark fear enveloped his heart, and he was drawn to face the summit once more; the beast had not yet claimed its prize.

As if in answer to his fears, the summit was plunged into holy white fire, and in that instant the Twisted Peak was judged by heaven's tribunal. The gods gathered around the summit block, each a crackling white pillar of light, and found it to be guilty of unforgiveable sin. And though the lowly stone screamed for grace, it was shown none. The beast that lurked in the shadows leapt out of the darkness with a tremendous clap and scorched the black stone with the blue whip of hell. Micah could bear the sight no longer. He lurched back into his descent. Behind him, alone on the summit, the Twisted Peak shrieked in agony.

The beast roared and vanished into the blackness. As Micah moved down the mountainside, he could feel it tasting the air for his flesh. The summit block was pittance, but Micah's soft body could be easily stripped aside, leaving his soul laid bare before the gods and exposed to white judgement and the fate of the Twisted Peak. His body flared in hot terror, inflating his body with a vast strength he had never known. Micah felt no pain as his body crashed against the black rock, for it was lost amongst the fear that coughed like smoke from his nostrils.

Out of the darkness the whip cracked relentlessly, probing the black peak for its champion. With every impact the mountain trembled, with every strike it was illuminated. But the world that sprung from the shadows made Micah pray for darkness. Below him trudged the towering hooded figures of the black gendarmes, bent forward in their toil for ascension. Their skeletal faces stretched gleefully as the gods answered their vengeful prayers. Micah ducked among the rocks each instance that the whip fell, for fear that the unholy procession might call out his hiding place to the monster that watched through the clouds.

59

Further down the mountain the air became heavy and damp and the rocks wet. A final snap of the whip overhead resounded, and with it the clouds spilled their contents over Micah's miserable head. The mountainside ran with water, and the loose talus slopes slicked with mud. Micah's legs sank into the ground, filling his boots with sticky earth and stone. His clothes clung wet and cold to his shivering frame and offered no warmth. Micah swam through darkness, utterly blind as even the light of the whip had retreated. The beast murmured from far away, then grew silent, leaving nothing but the hollow clatter of rain in its wake.

Divine light turned from the mountain, and in its absence a vacuum persisted. A great pressure mounted from within Micah's chest, and from it the fear which had cast him so forcefully from the summit seeped into the evening air. It left him not with relief, but a bitter soul that clawed frantically at his skin which had become an iron cavity in the numbing cold. A soul that demanded the retribution of the mountain; that lamented his cowardice and lowly descent of the summit. A soul that yearned to be in the presence of the gods, as had the Twisted Peak.

And Micah screamed at heaven, at the gods and the hound of justice. He screamed at the Twisted Peak, alone, lost amongst the ruin of its flanks. He screamed so that the soul which bled him from the inside might escape, to be free of its desires and destruction. But its claws continued to pull at his heart and at his mind. It tore at the memory of the valley, of home, and of family. It ravaged the secret joy of his heart at having escaped justice for his blasphemy, and instead called for more. Micah cried out in confusion and fell into tears, for he saw in that moment that the soul he had pursued was to be his tormenter.

Gradually the clouds were broken, and the rain ceased to fall. Micah gathered what little of himself remained on the forsaken peak and descended back through familiar terrain to the Three Finger Pass. He thought and felt very little as he travelled, his mind was numb with exhaustion. And so when he finally laid out his bedroll, his body thanked him for the chance at sleep.

CONVICTION

A life chosen of pursuit mandates conviction; the curious few are made seekers not by exception of intelligence, fortitude of spirit, or by merit of morality. Rather, the curious few are convicted by the promise of a greater potential in light of their own meager existence. The nature of curiosity provokes hope in that promise, and so armed with curiosity these made seekers probe for that potential. Some seekers stick their fingers into dark corners and are bitten. Of these, many will retreat supporting bloody digits. But few wrestle past the creatures in the shadow and are rewarded sparingly for their efforts. In fact, such rewards are so paltry that most still retreat in disgust, believing that greater potential a false construct. But fewer still cling to the scant reward, and realizing that it cannot satiate their longing are convicted more deeply of the great prize to be claimed. They are condemned to die without it.

For many long days passing clouds caught on the serrated edge of The Divide. The blade slit their soft bodies and deflated them into the narrow valleys that slipped craftily around the large summits. These valleys brimmed with gray corpses. Low shoulders between proud peaks overflowed, spilling their contents into adjacent gorges where the clouds ran like water. In this flow the wind whispered through the needles of sparsely grown trees, hushing the valley's denizens into stoic silence and promising to evict the sky's offspring from their resting places.

Into this world Micah had descended after having found shelter from the Twisted Peak. As he had swung himself over the northern edge of the Three Finger Pass, Micah felt not a tremor of emotion escape the prison of his heart. Nor had he felt strongly as he took his first steps into the carved depression below, his first steps within the body of The Divide. His mind simply retained the one objective it could recall, and shielded itself from the spite of his heart and soul.

So the days blurred in the fog, and Micah was bent forward by only the dim recollection of an intent. An intent that had been perverted by altitude; an intent that had eroded in the calamitous storm. And now as he let fall each weary step, that already beaten intent wasted away with his rations. His stomach protested loudly, and it gnawed at Micah's intellect. His last defense crumbled; cracks began to form letting poisonous fumes rise out of the depths of his consciousness. They came across his sinuses unexpectedly and tickled him out of trudging stupor, followed by sharp needles of regret and shame. They burrowed into his skin, indelicate reminders that his subconscious would not be subdued.

On one evening announced indiscriminately from evenings prior by the yellowing tint of the fog, Micah found himself walking idly over a plain of pale stone. He was awoken not by the now familiar pain of his body or of his subconscious, but by an unexpected touch of cold upon his toes. His mind took the cold only into simple consideration, but still prompted him to investigate further. Looking down, Micah saw that he had disturbed a little deposit of rainwater with his feet. Its surface writhed and contorted and sloshed upon the tiny banks of the stony indentation it inhabited. Micah watched with increasing interest as the pool began to settle, growing more comfortable with his presence after its initial display of indignation. He leaned in closer to the pool, and an absurd smile tugged at his lips as the surface coalesced.

As suddenly as the cold had touched his feet the pool collapsed into a golden window through which a stranger stared at Micah with wide eyes. It was an abhorrent creature, dirty and morose with features that hid behind an uneven growth of facial hair. It was a monstrous aggregation of flesh and bone that his mind, after some consideration, begrudgingly accepted as his own.

"So that has become the state of me," Micah whispered to the man behind the pane. "There before me stands a helpless victim of fear, wandering in the shroud of safety it has chosen for itself." He forced a confident grin, but the man only smiled weakly back. "See now the slave of fear, the greatest navigator of The Divide! See how easily he avoids its dangers, how easily he crosses its lowest passes! It is skillful, is it not? One might interpret from his movements that he has learned a mighty lesson, and has he not?" The ghoulish smile vanished. "Indeed he has. He has learned that there is no place among heaven for such humble constitution. He has learned that it is not choice but by gift of virtue that a man claims such a mighty passage." He observed eagerly as the man in the pool tasted his words, but to his surprise the man found them unfavorable.

"No?" Micah inquired. "Does a man not climb by virtue but by vice? How absurd!" Micah laughed with a sneer. "So he fancies himself a virtuous man still, and by that virtue he cannot ascend? A virtuous man indeed; my dear soul, virtue does not live in a cage. It is unbound, unfettered, unchained! And so it must be released from heavy bondage, and what stronger bond exists than the fear which coils like a venomous snake? No other bond can compare. It is clear that such a man should struggle at his chains and bleed at the wrists for the effort. It is no wonder that he appears before me broken and repugnant, he has relaxed in the stocks and resigned to their justice!"

The man in the pool trembled under his hot breath. "No, not a virtuous man indeed. Not a man at all, but a creature. For a man is free to choose, free to follow his soul even if it calls him to demise. Free to deny that same soul. But a creature is undercut by fear. A beast will entertain his passion only when there is nothing to fear.

"Still he does not find my words agreeable?" The man shook his head. "Is it that I've missed the mark, or that he dislikes illumination of his dark character?" Micah watched his reflection thoughtfully. The air was soft around him, the gray rock blended seamlessly into the thick sky. "Does he still then believe himself to be virtuous?" The man stared back without answer. "Without a doubt, he is bound by his fear. It is a fear that labors to preserve mortal flesh. Is it not that mortality by which the soul is set in opposition? And what of this soul that fights to escape me? What cruel humor it is to bind the immortal within a mortal frame! It would be better that I had been a beast, for a beast has nothing to withhold. Had I been a beast, knowing nothing of great endeavor, I should have been happily chained. I might find myself walking familiar meadows, kissed by the sun and blessed with the company of tender faces. Had I been a beast, I should never have betrayed that loyal company."

The man in the window shook with emotion. Bright troubled eyes peered out from behind tangle of hair. "But he has betrayed that company, he has valued his own soul over others. He allowed that soul to lead him by the nose to ascension, only to fall hopelessly short. Look now! Even as I speak of ascension I see him glow. Indeed, he is a great fool to think there is any path to the gods short of the City."

No sooner had Micah finished his words than the clouds behind the man ruptured, revealing for a moment the stone-clad armor of a mighty sentinel of The Divide. Its sheer vertical face dominated the hole in the clouds, polished clean by the abuse of the seasons. Involuntarily, a gasp left Micah's lips, and he spun to take in the sight directly. But he merely caught a glimpse of the sentinel before it slipped behind a gray curtain.

"Dearest soul, you deny my basic instincts. Why should such heights tempt me, for I know in my heart and mind they promise only death? And yet, I became alive the moment I stepped foot upon its ruinous slope! Even now I am captivated by its cousin; I yearn to touch the lonely summit, to stand so auspiciously is to satiate the ego of my hungry soul!"

The man in the pool longed silently for another visit from the tall sentinel. He gazed into the space it had occupied. "I wonder the thoughts that pass through the minds of all who have climbed to such heights. I wonder that I, so divided in mind and soul, should ever chance at their glory. I wonder that it is my very mind which has hobbled my soul."

Micah did not return to the pool. His mind gently loosed its grip, and allowed him to stumble away into the fog.

FEAR

It is the fate of the seeker to become burdened by clairvoyance. Though intrinsically a man of action, the seeker settles easily into the role of the passive. For the seeker sees the world peeled, and is paralyzed by fear. He watches as his infant brother fearlessly places a fat hand into the fire, only to be toted away by a scolding father. But when the seeker then merely teases the flame with a timid finger, he finds that his family has left the room, and that he sits alone. And so he is left beside the fire to covet his brothers scorched fingers, and to hate his healthy own.

After Micah left the pool he wandered into the night, unconscious of the physical world and deaf to the wailing of his soul. But even his ignorance could not dissuade his body from collapse, and so he soon sprawled across the stone in a heavy sleep. And as Micah slept, The Divide drew a mighty breath and blew the gray visitors from its passages. They made no complaint as they slid along, but the drag of their slippery bodies licked the rock with morning dew. After they had gone The Divide again breathed normally and waited for the sun to rise.

Micah was awakened by the drying of his face which was basked in mid-morning light. He squinted as an unfamiliar yellow bloom danced between opaque towers on a high ridge to the east. The sun touched his face but had yet to penetrate the shadow of the valley that lingered over the remainder of his damp body. Eager, Micah clambered to his feet and spread his arms above his head. He turned himself slowly like game on a spit, letting his skin drink in warmth. In the light he forgot his hunger, forgot his misgivings, let go of his pain. It departed with the morning dew.

The valley glowed like fire in the rising light, its many pools and rivers luminescent by the warm kiss of the sun. It was a perfectly carved trough of stone in which a growth of vibrant green ran down its throat and sloshed gently onto steep retaining walls. These walls were broken periodically by gushing falls sourced by the tears of the tall sentinels. They towered over the valley on either side, shuffling in shoulder to shoulder like jealous siblings. Each hid its cherished summit out of sight of those that stood humbly below.

With the dawn Micah found renewed inspiration to hunt, and was rewarded handsomely for his efforts. By midday his stomach was quiet, and his mind was once again free of physical perturbations. Micah followed the gurgling rivers downstream, idling occasionally to watch as small clouds met their demise in collision with thorny peaks. He still knew little of his destination, but took some solace in that the valley ran generally northward. Navigating the bush and stone was slow, but Micah enjoyed the simple distraction. He walked for most of the day in great spirits, unblemished by any despairing voice from his soul.

The gorge through which Micah walked found juncture with another, far more expansive valley that ran north-easterly. Micah spied it early as he descended beside the riverbed. Close to this intersection Micah was forced to negotiate rocky terrain over which the river pooled and plummeted. Carefully picking his way along the cliffs, he managed to arrive safely at the bottom, where he found that the river ran quickly to join its kin. The new valley was flat and wide. It flowed with short alpine grass, and only carried a concentration of pale trees around a primary river. The river was a culmination of the tears of adjacent peaks, it moved white and heavy as it carried away the winter burden of The Divide. It was more powerful than any river Micah had seen before.

To Micah's delight, the new valley supported a distinct trail that followed adjacent to the river. Beaming, he gained stone marker after marker, and his progress gained considerable momentum. The path was well trodden, his footsteps joined many others both young and old that had left soft depressions in the soil. The trail could be seen distinctly for a great distance, as the valley hardly deviated in its direction. It was broken only by the occasional conglomeration of short, woody trees that congested the river's tributaries.

As the sun began its slow descent over the western ridge of the valley, Micah began to notice a consistent pair of tracks in the soil. The further he walked the more pronounced they became. The tracks were of small form and moved unevenly; he found that he could not easily match stride with them due to their irregular pattern. His curiosity prompted him to move more quickly in hopes that he might gain the owner of the odd tracks.

Micah was walking amidst a growth of trees when the sound of shuffling feet tickled his ears. He froze, and verified that the source was not his own. The sound was faint, but undeniable. Micah sprang forward despite mounting apprehension. Not only did he desire to see another face, but he realized that he burned with curiosity to witness a true citizen of The Divide. Micah blundered past branches and leapt over stones, he splashed through snowmelt and turned each corner of the trail wildly. And in a flash of sunlight he burst from the grove into the open blue sky.

The wind hummed through the grass. The path cut a sharp line in the alpine meadow, straight and narrow. It ran north. Micah was still, rooted to the soil. Not ten paces from him a bent, hooded figure brandished a crude blade in one wrinkled hand. The figure held Micah in stiff regard, offering nothing but the promise of sharpened steel. Micah merely gaped in return, his words had escaped him. His lips were dry, and his tongue staled. Despite himself, he was resigned to stand mutely and await the judgement of the hooded figure.

The figure was comfortable to scrutinize Micah from afar. After long consideration, the blade arm was relaxed and the figure took a few awkward steps forward. Micah immediately recognized the unusual gait as he had followed it for the greater portion of the day.

"Not a beast, not a man, but a boy." The figure returned the blade to a sheath concealed within the folds of its cloak. It then extended both hands, gripped the hood which masked its face, and drew the cloth back slowly. From within its shadow the smiling face of an old woman emerged. Micah's surprise bloomed on his face like the afternoon sun, to which the old woman's smile widened.

"Expecting a man? Pray tell, which man do you seek? You are lucky that you are so noisy, I might have gutted you for sneaking up on me otherwise!" Her voice was as bronzed as the complexion of her skin, and carried the same deeply chiseled wrinkles.

"I am- I am not seeking anyone at all," Micah stammered. "But I saw your footsteps, and I wanted to meet you."

"You would be wise to mind your own business; most mountain folk do not take kindly to strangers." Her eyes flashed. "But one from the valley can easily recognize another."

"You are from the valley, the same that is south of The Divide?" A seed of disappointment escaped him. The old woman drew her mouth tightly. A flurry of wind nipped at her skin, and her features withdrew into a forest of tight wrinkles. Micah shivered, but the old woman bore her leathered skin like armor. "Surely you cannot be from the valley," he gasped through the chill. "I have seen none such as yourself!"

The wind settled, and the old woman emerged from her shell. She waived his words aside. "I have spent seasons in the valley, and seasons abroad. I traversed these mountains before taking residence in the valley, and now after many long seasons I have returned. I am no stranger to them, if that is your concern," she added as an afterthought.

"I never doubted it! But I wonder, what brings you into The Divide, for I see that you have no wares, and surely this is not a place for the elderly."

"And do you suppose that you are much more adept than I?" The woman smiled again, but her voice was sharp. "What good can a young and foolish boy do that this old body cannot?"

Micah was incredulous. "You have a limp, surely the travel must be painful! How can you expect to overcome the wrath of the gods who have cursed this wretched land? This is not a place for the weak!"

The old woman raised a wizened brow. "So you are among the strong?"

"Bless the gods, no!" Micah's heart beat heavily in his chest; he was consumed by a sudden swell of emotion that could not be levied. But so earnest was his feeling that he was not ashamed to speak openly.

"Good," the old woman said simply. "I don't much like the strong. They don't truly live in the mountains." Micah's incredulity leaked across his face. "Not like you or I, child." The woman's voice slipped into a whisper as she hobbled forward, searching Micah with her eyes. She suddenly froze, finding what she sought. "We know that there is much to be afraid of here."

"Whatever do you mean, old woman?" Micah's voice cracked. "We do not deserve to be here, we cannot survive! By all means of wisdom, we should return home!"

"By all means of wisdom," the old woman cackled. "You mean to advise me, do you? Let your wisdom speak to this: if the child is so wise, why does he walk further north?"

Micah's mind spun, he struggled to procure an answer over the screaming of his heart. He resigned to glare at the old woman, biting his lip.

"You don't wish to tell? Ah, the child does not yet know!" The old woman laughed. "Perhaps my great age does bear with it a gem of wisdom, though you may be the judge. Let me tell you a story of when I was young.

"Many seasons ago, I met a great climber while walking in the lowest valley of the Southern Range. He was a tall man, built powerfully, weathered by the four seasons and hardened by altitude. I found him, or rather, he found me, as he easily overcame me on the winding trail. You see, even in those days I was blessed with infirmity, my legs had grown crooked as a child. The man was kind, and stopped to prepare me a meal as I was low on provisions. We ate together that evening, and our conversation naturally settled on our business in those mountains.

"The man was no trapper, no trader, he had no title save for climber. He lived in those mountains, for those mountains. And he had conquered so many summits, that surely none like him have ever since walked that trail. He regaled me with tales of his mighty ascents, of the paramount beauty of his summits, and of their harrowing descents. He had seen death; he had thwarted its cold hand many times. He had been touched by the blue judgement of the gods and was not found guilty.

"As I listened to his stories, a single question began to take hold of me. And so I asked him, 'surely one who has climbed to such great heights has no place in such a low valley; why is it that we have met at a place so unbefitting?'

"He heard my question, and gave his answer with a smile. 'Truthfully, it is not the summit alone that I seek. Indeed, one might very easily confuse one summit with another. It is a poor prize. No, the summit alone is not enough. It needs another, it needs its partner. It needs to stand beside its humble brother, the low valley, and only then can it claim any glory. Why do I walk the lowest valley? I tell you, it is so that I can ascend from it the mightiest peak! And when I have done so, I might also take part in the purest glory of the heavens!'

"A fire burned in his eyes. The next day he left me to walk the low valley alone, for he intended to claim his prize. But I did not see him again. Now child, please tell me this: what do you think of his answer?"

The old woman waited expectantly. Micah, though still flustered, had managed to regain some composure while she talked.

"He was a man of strength."

"He was a fool," she spat.

"I do not know your purpose, and I will not guess it for I suspect that it is madness," Micah immediately retorted. "Your story means nothing, and you criticize the very spirit of the mountains within which you walk!"

Micah made an attempt to sidestep the old woman on the trail, but in an instant she had procured her blade and blocked his movements. Micah was furious, but his fear restrained him.

"I cannot let you leave child, not until you have listened." The old woman wore a mask of knotted flesh.

"I am listening," Micah pleaded.

"Good," she nodded. "Listen well. For it is true that I have never climbed a great peak, I have never felt the summit

70

beneath my lame feet, though it beckoned. And my every step is pain, my prospects are dire. Do you not think that I too fear? But the mighty climber, he did not know pain as I have. He did not fear the mountains as I do. And yet, he fabricated his pain, invented that fear. For what purpose? I tell you, that great man would have traded his body for mine should I had offered it to him. For in his heart of hearts, the strong man desires to be weak. Remember child, the weak are easily punished, but the gifts of the soul are unknown to the strong."

When the old woman finished speaking, she slid the blade back into its sheath and shuffled aside from the trail. She did not take her eyes from Micah's.

"Madness," Micah mumbled. He then raised his voice as he marched by the old woman on the trail, "I wish to you the best, though I am afraid this land will not be kind to either of us." He did not look back, even when the sound of shuffling feet was once again carried to him by the wind. Soon, it faded and was lost.

III. the White Mountain

COMPANIONSHIP

For long has the seeker been alone in the woods; long have the curious wandered to the far corners of the world. It is a lonely burden, and soon becomes too great to bear. The few always become fewer in time. A slight deviation from the trail, a coy whisper in the ear, it is enough to lure the few into the temptations of others. To see in others that which does not exist, or has already been lost. As the seeker cannot bear his burden alone, so easily he does offer it to those who are unworthy. They find it unsavory. It is cast aside, forgotten in the dust of the miserable road.

The words of the old woman rattled between Micah's ears long after he had left her beside the trail. He offered them to the scrutiny of his mind, but it found them unfavorable. They fell though like scattered parchment only to catch fire on the coals of his heart. Micah brimmed with anger until the last of her words had been consumed by the flame. They could not escape the fire; they could not reach his soul.

By nightfall Micah felt clean of her speech, and in the morning hardly recalled their brief encounter. He picked up his belongings and fell back into the toil of the old trail, though the movements were of no cost to his spirit. The mighty valley was capped with tall mountains, each as inviting as they were terrible to behold. Each whispered seductively to his soul. Micah frequently found himself scrutinizing the stony faces, probing for points of weakness, struggling to identify the high summits. He craned his neck and perched on his toes, only to be flushed as he realized its futility.

Every morning as the sun crested the eastern lip of the valley, he pledged to challenge the noblest peak on the horizon. Every morning a greater peak was laced with gold on the high ridge, flashing a chiseled ramp or jagged ridge or crumbling face that led to a summit enflamed with the dawn fire that guarded the most precious gift of immortality. In those moments Micah was consumed with hope for he remembered no weakness and recalled no notion of righteous terror. The mountain became his motivation, the only target worthy of his craving soul. But the dawn always turns to dusk, and Micah's flame cooled in the evening air. Golden faces rolled down their black shrouds; the dawn fire choked and was lost into dark clouds. The summit of promise and light was now an abysmal tomb that dared his approach. Micah forgot his vow in the dying light, and remembered his fear. As he made camp he shuddered to think he had once contemplated such slopes.

In such a conundrum Micah spent many days traveling the old trail. The valley continued to lean north. With each passing of the sun the valley revealed ever nobler a battlement that protected its embankments. Atop these fortifications rode the Knights of The Divide. The earliest guards were but stony flesh riddled with cancerous protrusions as their own bodies besieged them; the head of each grew from the back of its neighbor. But as Micah walked, the Knights changed. They straightened their shoulders, pointed their chins, and began to march in formation. No longer did they stand naked, but instead donned sparkling helms of ice. They ushered Micah through the valley as if to pay homage to an illustrious king. Though Micah was sorely tempted by the glittering Knights, his fears were no longer the chain which kept him grounded. Instead the intoxicating desire to see what treasure The Divide hid within its bosom drove him ever onwards.

Many tight valleys emptied into the expanse in which Micah walked. Of these, several contained trails of their own. Micah began to notice the crusted tracks below him were no more, replaced by the moist imprints of booted feet and cloven hoof. Although his previous encounter with the denizens of The Divide had made him wary of chance meetings, Micah still harbored a desire to interact with another traveler. He did, however, resolve to not be on the receiving end of a surprise encounter, and so was especially alert during travel.

Micah had been tracking a particularly fresh set of tracks when the sun slipped over the west lip of the valley. Plunged in rapid darkness, Micah decided to break camp in a large grove. The moon graciously accompanied the stars and allowed Micah to fumble with his tarpaulin without the necessity of a torch. Micah rarely produced fire as he was increasingly afraid of compromising his position near the trail. He succeeded in erecting a crude shelter, and braced himself inside for a cold sleep.

Micah was nearing sleep when a nearby sound tickled his senses. His eyes snapped open, and his head cocked north in the direction of the perturbation. Now vigilant, his ears caught the bark of laughter ringing off the trunks of the grove. Micah scrambled out of his shelter and searched the darkness with blind eyes until he caught an unmistakable flicker of light dancing through the thicket north of his encampment. He dropped low, and watched the fire with rising unease. It remained rooted, not a torch but a campfire serving a small host of travelers. Despite his reservations, Micah could not remain comfortably at his site and felt compelled to gain the advantage. He removed his boots, and crept barefoot through a tangled web of barren trees, all the while with ears keen on sampling the company's dialogue.

"Fill that idiot's cup so that he might have something to stifle his laughter," a thick voice scolded from beside the fire.

"Aye John, fill me cup and I'll no longer be merry, for even the priest knows that temperance is the shortest path to unruliness!" The second voice was slobbering and high, sprinkled with fits of giggling.

A third voice answered, "Is it wise? I think he grows unrulier as he drinks."

"Of course he does," the first voice bit back. "But he holds less mead than my mother. Let the jester drown in his favorite drink, I say."

Micah had arrived at the fringe of the light scattered by the fire, keeping well concealed behind a large boulder. He could now distinguish each of the three: one glared disapprovingly at another who lay dangerously close to the campfire with his naked torso exposed, enjoying reprieve from the cold while simultaneously dredging deep from the metal tankard that he gripped in both hands. The third sat on the other side of the fire, nearest to Micah. All wore the leather of trappers, and all were armed at the hip with sabers except the second, whose weapon was flung carelessly from the fire. Micah eyed the steel nervously.

"Drown in his drink," the second voice exclaimed, belonging to the trapper that lay by the fire. "Why, it's the death I've always wanted! Not indeed to meet the sharp end of the sword such as yourself, O mighty Bernard the Brave, once a Shearer of Sheep now risen to Tanner of Tiny Woodland Creatures! I remember the day you earned the title; lo, the teeth of the dread lord marmot could not penetrate thy tempered bracer, try as he might! Our father would be proud to hear such titles, would he not?" Chuckling, the man threw his head back and brought the tankard to his lips.

The owner of the first voice was not amused. His face purpled noticeably through the flickering light of the fire. Without a moment's consideration he took a swift stride and promptly levelled a kick into the tankard, sending it with its contents sputtering into the fire.

"I hear no great titles surrounding you, Claudius! Jester, clown, fool!" He spat into the dirt.

Claudius stared into the empty space between his hands before dropping them dejectedly. "A great pity. Now I will surely wake the entire valley with my fits of laughter. O hubris, you have doomed us all!"

"Please, do not raise your voice; we do not know what walks in the night!" The third voice, belonging to the seated man, made no attempt to conceal the plea in his voice. Claudius studied him, and sighed.

"For you John, I concede my tomfoolery. Though let it be known it was not to save the righteous neck of my brother." He turned his face from Bernard in mock disgust but could not subdue a smirk. Bernard mimicked the gesture, but no smile trifled his lips. The company locked in stiff silence, though Claudius appeared apathetic to it. He proceeded to prod his tankard from the fire using a long stick, humming to himself for the duration of the process. Micah waited uncomfortably in the darkness. He did not dare make any movement should his stirring break the stillness, despite the numbness that crept between his toes.

To John, the quiet seemed too much to bear. He shifted nervously, "Now where has he gone off to? The fire is getting dark."

Bernard tossed the remains of their woodpile into the flame and shrugged. "Out watching the mountains grow, no doubt forgotten all about the firewood."

"And they call me a fool!" Claudius poking the tankard with a bare finger to test its heat. He yelped and popped the blistering finger into his mouth. Bernard, watching his brother, tried at great lengths to swallow a chuckle but failed. Even John was tickled; his shoulders bobbed in noiseless laughter.

Silence still threatened the air, and John once again interrupted the lonely crackle of the fire. "Why does he do it, Bernard?"

"How should I know? Do you see me watching them?"

Claudius gave the tankard another nudge and was pleased with the result. "There's no vermin atop the spires for my dear brother to slay, John," he grinned.

"The fool is right," Bernard consented. "They hold nothing for me, and as such I do not stare. Perhaps there is some prize for him up there?"

"Perhaps," John murmured. He looked up from the fire to search for the ridgeline, but it was lost in the night. "I see nothing but fear in those towers," he shuddered.

"Fear?" Claudius simpered. He too turned to the horizon, but his eyes were blind beside the fire. "I see no reason to be afraid. Let the giants stand on their pedestals; my desire places both feet in the sand!" For effect, Claudius pressed wriggling toes into the soil.

"Our business concerns no gods and no tall towers, young John. You should put such fear aside, for it distracts and is unmanly," Bernard said with folded arms. Great delight splashed across Claudius' face.

"*Young* John," Claudius savored, letting the words hang in the air and noting his brother's irate expression. "Heed our timeless wisdom. Look not to the west or the east, but to the north and south! Let no siren that overlooks the valley strike fear into thy youthful heart. For there is coin to be made and spent in the valley, trifles to enjoy, and pleasures to indulge!"

"You have never been a man to speak wisdom Claudius, in the short time we have travelled together. I find it difficult to believe that you should start now!"

All three travelers twisted in unison to identify the sudden fourth voice that had sprung from the shadows. Micah's heart leapt, for the voice had been borne not ten paces from his hiding place. Instinct drove Bernard' hand to the hilt of his sabre, but he allowed it to slip when the owner of the voice strode into the firelight.

The fourth traveler was hooded in wool unlike the three trappers, and carried a large bundle of sticks knotted behind his back. He cast the bundle beside the fire, and sat heavily beside John who appeared to still be recovering from shock.

"I am glad you have not forgotten the firewood, Mountain-Gazer," Claudius teased.

"Mountain-Gazer," the fourth repeated with a smile in his voice. "What have I done to warrant this new infamy?"

Bernard snorted. "Why, you have earned the title many times over. It is perhaps the most appropriate title issued from my brother's mouth."

The fourth companion laughed. "I must confess; I am partial to it. So what if I am guilty, it is largely the purpose for this guileless mission after all."

"For you perhaps," Claudius sniffed. "But what of the other traveler, Micah, was it? Is he not a piece to fit your puzzle?"

Micah froze. He had been in the process of meticulous retreat when the second companion uttered his name. His mind began to turn slowly, thick as a wagon wheel churning through clay.

"That may be left for chance to decide, though I am young in trusting such unreasonable things." The fourth traveler's voice was a thread that caught upon the spokes of Micah's mind.

Claudius threw his arms wide in a welcoming gesture. "It is good to hear you finally embrace my god! She may be blind, but she is sensual, is she not?"

"My friend, you should be wary to welcome a blind god into your camp. Hear the wisdom of the Mountain-Gazer, for unlike the trappers he has learned to see!"

"Hardly," Bernard interjected. "The trapper is little without his sight."

The fourth traveler raised a triumphant finger. "Then it is my duty to report that none of you should bear the title! For it was I, not the trapper, who has seen the one who lingers in the darkness!"

Bernard was again red in the face. "Speak not in riddles, we have one who does so already!"

"Look not to me, this riddle is beyond me," Claudius admitted curiously.

"Then I'll be frank. While you three have bickered about the fireplace another has taken vigil nearby. By those boulders, over there. He means no harm- I daresay he is not even armed. But it is unsettling that seasoned trappers such as yourselves should not have noticed."

The fourth companion cast an incriminating thumb in the direction of Micah's hiding place, and all four turned in his direction. Micah blanched. A bolt of energy flashed in his legs and the ratcheting gears of his mind burst into a spinning frenzy. He bolted from his hiding place and crashed through the trees without as much as a backwards glance. Through the cloud of the animal that seized him he heard Bernard shout, followed by the snapping of branches. The snapping closed in, and Micah became acutely aware of a steady breath over his shoulder. Terror was insufficient to save him from his pursuer, and he felt powerful hands seize his arm. Micah contorted his body but could not escape, the hands pulled sharply and Micah's sprinting legs abandoned the support of his torso. He landed square on the flat of his back.

Bernard stood over Micah with a wide smile. His sabre was drawn, and he poised it just shy of Micah's quivering throat. "I have him!" he shouted back to the camp. No voice answered, but Claudius could be heard regaling the other travelers of his brother's great stamina. Bernard turned back to his prize, gripped Micah firmly by the neck, and hoisted him to his feet. Together they marched back to the campsite.

Although Micah was wholly compliant, Bernard deemed it necessary to jab his prisoner occasionally with the tip of his sabre. When they reached the fire Bernard brought Micah to his knees with a blow.

"Traveler? Trader? Thief?" Bernard lingered on the latter accusation.

"Traveler!" Micah gasped. "I mean no-," but Micah's words never left his throat. The fourth companion stood before him. Their eyes locked in recognition.

"Micah, can it be?" The fourth companion exclaimed.

"Zachary!" Micah breathed at long last. He lifted an unsteady foot, and stood. Bernard made no attempt to stop him. Of the three, only Claudius put together the pieces quickly enough.

"This is the one? The one who lurks in the shadows? Mountain-Gazer, what strange friends you entertain! And I must express my utter disappointment, for he is no inspiration to behold."

Zachary ignored him. "Micah, it is good to see you again, and how unexpected!" They embraced arms, sharing warm smiles. Micah was bewildered and he failed to reciprocate the greeting, but he could not help but grin at the familiar face. Zachary's face showed evidence of a similar sentiment, though his words did not escape him. "I had not anticipated seeing you so soon, for I believed you would be days ahead! Tell me, why is it that you are still here? Did you lose the trail? Or perhaps...," he trailed off, searching Micah's face for the clue that he suspected. It was found in the long shadows that played over his face, hiding from illumination by the flame. It was found trembling behind pallor eyes.

"Did you summit?"

"Yes."

The fire crackled, sending tiny points of light gliding into the night sky only to be swallowed by the darkness. A spark twirled around Zachary's head and found refuge under his cowl. But as it smoldered, Micah could see through Zachary's eyes an old ember flicker and burn. Zachary was silent, his face stretched thin. It danced in the light.

"The gods were furious in those days," he whispered. "Why Micah, why did you do it? Why did you tempt them?" He didn't wait for an answer, but only continued with growing fervor. "What did you see?"

"I saw The Divide. From the summit I shared the clouds of all the mighty peaks. And I saw the jealously of the gods, Zachary. I saw the Twisted Peak punished with my own eyes. I saw those who exact justice on the tall mountains of The Divide."

"Mountain-Climber," Claudius proposed quietly. Then, with enthusiasm, "Mountain-Climber! I see now the puzzle, isn't it plain? Mountain-Gazer, witness the Mountain-Climber! He surely is an inspiration, though he lurks in shadows, for who sees the mountain closer than he who scrambles over its very stone? So that is why you strike out into The Divide, not to gaze, but to feel! Not to skitter through the low valley such as us unmoral trappers, but to frolic over its highest battlements! To be a conqueror! Yes, I see the desire, I see the tug, to be as the gods themselves, righteous and mighty!"

Claudius jumped to his feet and clasped a friendly hand on both Zachary and Micah's shoulders. "Noble climber," he addressed Micah, and then turned to Zachary and appended, "Aspiring conqueror. Allow me to join your legions, for I too seek the holy path. Though my brother may show skepticism, as John can attest I've been yearning release from my wanton ways. And I see no better freedom from my iniquities than to lock them in a case of ice and snow!" His eyes glinted mischievously. "Better yet, allow me cast myself from the highest mountain, such that my wicked soul be scattered across the mountainside. For by denying myself my safety, my pleasures, my body, I will surely gain the glory of heaven!" Claudius swooped down to John and wrapped an encouraging arm around his shoulders. "For that immortal gift *young* John, is truly the greatest gift a mortal creature can receive."

His speech concluded, Claudius waited as if a performer for applause. When he received nothing but a look of disdain from his brother, he sighed mightily. "But it is all in jest. You both will surely die." Claudius faced away from the fire, and feigning injury to his dignity marched into the woods.

Bernard watched him leave with contempt. "Always a buffoon. My brother tells nothing but lies. But Zachary, why this man? This is a worm that hides in darkness. It would be best to put a sword in his stomach and leave him for the wolves. Better to let him die here than by letting him blaspheme the gods."

Zachary gave no answer. Bernard grunted, and furrowed his brow. "Fine. You have given us enough guidance into The Divide. Should you wish to continue with our party, so be it. But if you want to keep company with this man," he gave a curt nod towards Micah, "then know that you will no longer be welcome with us. We don't need another member to feed, especially one who is inclined to hide in darkness."

"Then I'll be leaving your party," Zachary responded immediately. "Thank you Bernard for your protection and companionship. Be safe John, I wish you the best in your career." Zachary again grasped Micah by the arm. "Micah, do you have a camp nearby? I would gladly join you, if you would allow me."

"Yes, of course! I welcomed your company once, and I would not deny it now!" Micah was overjoyed. Together they gathered Zachary's belongings, and with a final farewell departed the campsite. They walked without speaking at first, each attempting to process the sudden turn of events. But Micah could not bear the silence for long, for he was boiling with questions.

"Zachary, is it as Claudius says, why you have crossed The Divide?"

"Nothing that Claudius says is true." Zachary hesitated, then continued slowly. "But I did not cross for gold, or for pleasure. I crossed because I did not speak truthfully to you when we last met. I'm afraid that I am a slave to my heart, Micah. The Divide sung to me the evening you departed, and all it took was to see you answer that call. I could not sleep, I struggled to eat. Suddenly my home had become a prison, a coffin in which to die. It was unbearable, and despite all of my reason I knew that I had to go." He stopped walking, and turned to face Micah. "I was afraid." There was shame in his voice, and his eyes failed to meet Micah's. "It was not until I met those three passing through my home that I had the courage to venture into The Divide. I would not have done it alone."

They began to walk again. Micah's campsite was near. Before they reached the site, another question brimmed to the surface of Micah's mind. It was a question that he had asked himself many times before.

"When we look at them, why are we afraid?"

"Is it not a fear of death and of divine justice?"

"But why then does Claudius not feel afraid, why does Bernard not fear the mountains? Surely they would be judged more harshly than we."

Zachary thought for a moment. "They have no reason to fear. They will never tempt the mountains, and they know it."

"What of John, for he too is afraid? Will he ever challenge them?"

"I do not think it. But it is not my place to know."

They arrived at the campsite, and constructed an additional shelter for Zachary. They talked for great length into the night, each delighting in the others account of The Divide. The morning was near approaching when they were finally overcome with sleep.

PURPOSE

The few are not lost, but have found one another. They hold each other close; they are desperate for a similar heart. A heart that beats as their own. And in the light of the other their own search will bloom into question. For the few are passionate, and that passion alone is blinding. But the same passion that casts a bright glare into the eye of the individual is quick to illuminate the corpse of purpose in another.

As the sun rose in the new day the two companions regained the old trail with a renewed vigor, bolstered by each's company. The Divide became the sole object of their discourse; it was total and all-consuming. Together they imagined each summit, together they traced routes to the heavens. They were children again, laughing and marveling at the wonders of the ancient world. And as the sun faded and the darkness reigned, their wonder did not fade. It was not stuck down by fear, for the face of courage in each other was enough to forget such troubles.

They continued north, and along the valley each Knight they passed was more decorated than the last. The Knights now bore vast breastplates of ice. They wielded ornate swords with hilts of solid rock and splintering blades glazed by sparkling frost. The Knights faced north.

"Zachary, you have heard tales of The Divide. For whom do they wait?" Micah nodded towards the tall sentinels.

"You do not know?" Zachary expressed genuine surprise. "I should have thought it would be common knowledge even in the valley. Micah, we walk in the Hall of the White Mountain."

His word was reverent, spoken softly. They stood on a rock outcropping that rose above the river. It offered an unbroken view of the valley and its mighty guard. At the base of the valley the river ran wide and blue, surrounded by a pale green; it was a struggle for foliage to prosper in the enduring cold. It eventually faded to gray near to the inclining walls, and as the walls rose the stone was tucked under a white crust of snow. The crest of the valley could not be seen, for the white summits crumbled and revealed vast arteries of crystalline blue that bled into the azure sky.

"It is the first I have heard of it," Micah admitted.

"It is the most holy offering of The Divide. See how the peaks pay tribute? Micah, I told no lie when I warned you of the Twisted Peak. That is a most unholy pinnacle, eternally scarred by the gods. But the White Mountain, it is all the Twisted Peak is not. The gods have found favor in its purpose, and so it is spared from their judgement. The White Mountain is said to be the most beautiful summit of The Divide. It is said to be wider than the Hall itself, it is said to split the sky as a pyramid."

Micah felt a familiar tongue of heat fan into flame within his chest. "What of its summit, Zachary? What have you heard?"

"That it is blessed."

"Blessed!" Micah repeated in awe.

"Yes. That it is blessed by the gods themselves, such that any mortal who gains it may share in the blessing. For it is said that only he who shares its purpose may reach the summit."

"Purpose," Micah wondered. "What purpose do the tall mountains have Zachary, but to challenge the gods themselves and take residence in heaven? Though I have summited but one of the creatures of The Divide, I have seen naught but damnation. And the Twisted Peak was but a low and miserable rock, if the gods could not forgive it's jealously how could they forgive that of a taller peak? Surely its purpose is to claim a seat beside the gods, and surely such desire could only be fueled by the greater wretchedness of its soul!"

Zachary raised an eyebrow. "Is that what you think of it then, the burning of our souls? Is that what the Twisted Peak has taught you? I must admit that I have not had the experience as you Micah, for I have only listened to tales. But this fire I have finally entertained, no, I do not believe it to be wicked. For though I doubt myself even now, I cannot deny the way my body sung when I placed a hesitant foot onto the stairway to the Three Finger Pass. I can no longer deny my soul, though for so many seasons I have tried."

"But why Zachary does the soul desire it? Bernard, Claudius, they had only worldly passions. Are they wicked for not wanting more, or is it we who are as guilty as the Twisted Peak? We are mortal, Zachary. What business do we have on the high summits?"

"It is a question I have not answered, Micah." Zachary's crooked teeth slipped out from behind drawn lips. "I hope to answer it when at last I have conquered a holy summit. And though now you protest your soul, I have no doubt that we will answer this question together!"

Micah nodded, and chose his words with care. "You say that the Twisted Peak is unholy. For surely as I have climbed the Twisted Peak and seen what is unrighteous in its purpose, I will climb this White Mountain and learn the holy path. Zachary, will you join me? Together, if it is as you say, we too may be blessed by the gods. And if such a blessing is mere knowledge to our questions, then so be it! I am eager to put the cravings of my soul to rest."

Zachary grinned, but a slight shadow furrowed in his brow. "Do you think it wise, Micah, for one such as myself to try such a peak now? I am not tried as you are; I am afraid that my body may not yet be strong enough. I am afraid that my soul may not yet be strong enough."

Micah laughed. "Dear friend, you are a man of The Divide, are you not? You are seasons more tried than I, and your body since birth has been tempered by stone! As for your soul, I could not hope to climb with a more noble heart. For if the gods do exact justice upon us, it will surely be I that they find guilty. They will remember the stench of my soul as it cowers upon the rocks." Micah's laughter had ceased.

The river roared from below their perch. It foamed crested white waves as it was pushed violently from the heart of The Divide. It was as cold as blue ice. Zachary placed an encouraging hand on Micah's shoulder, and thumped his chest with vigor. "You remind me of my nature, and I thank you. I am a child of the Twisted Peak, and long have I known its cruelty. And you Micah," he rapped Micah's chest with a clenched fist. "You have ascended its flanks! You have met the same evil it endures, and you have survived! Micah, the gods do not exact justice idly. If you had been found guilty, you would not have left the mountain." He took a step back, and raised his arms questioningly. "What of the White Mountain? It is a holy peak; its purpose is just. We seek the answers to our souls; what more holy and just a purpose is there? I tell you, there is none. Even if our souls were wicked, to seek truth there is no greater purpose. Let us find the White Mountain, let us reach the summit, for surely then we will be satisfied!"

The river sparkled. The carpet that traced the Hall of the White Mountain was as blue as the sky. Micah lifted downcast eyes, and searched the horizon. "Yes," he breathed. He shouldered his pack, and Zachary followed suit. "How much further until we reach the White Mountain?"

"I cannot say for certain, though from what I recall it should be less than five days' walk."

"Then let us be off Zachary, for our purpose is just and it is holy! Surely it is the will of the gods that has brought us together, for together we will find peace with our souls."

Together, they regained the trail.

LOVE

Now at last the wandering few come together, for truth has a natural gravity. Such a prize attracts suitors, though their love is fickle and their passions polluted. Nevertheless, as each has broken the tide and weathered the storm and refused to dismiss their deepest desire, they will not abandon it now. Though they may not yet understand it, the lonely seeker is soon to die, and the lover born.

No trees grew so close to the center of The Divide. It was a place of tundra. It was a landscape of rock cut from the mountainsides. The wind never ceased in such a place; it wailed in the evenings and whispered in the mornings. And if the wind were to grow still, if only for an instant, nothing but the distant rumble of snow collapsing under a high noon sun would fill the void. The valley became an empty place, a giant's road crumbling save for the ancient trail that weaved through the cracks.

As Zachary and Micah followed the trail north, they began to see more signs of other travelers. Soon they found that they shared the trail; merchants and traders, trappers and journeymen, they began to pass each as they walked the long path. Some were friendly, some ignored their presence, and others threatened with hard expressions and iron. They came from the many adjoining trails in the valley, from cities within and far beyond the walls of The Divide. But those who walked north did so with a set jaw and white knuckles. They gripped layers of leather and wool tightly to their bodies. Many wore masks of skin not unlike the leathered goods they promised to sell. The youth of each party was marked by the blistering red of his face. Both Micah and Zachary shared in the mark.

But not all who walked the trail moved north; there were some who descended the path. Though many of these were much of the same in outward appearance as the northward travelers, Micah saw something in each of their faces that was quite unlike anything he had seen before. He only caught a fleeting glimpse of each as the wind fluttered and drew back their cowls; it was enough to make out what was unmistakable. He saw a softness in their cheeks, he saw their eyes open wide. Their lips moved silently, slowly. They had seen the White Mountain.

"It must be close now. See now one of them returns from the north; I shall ask him how far we have left to travel."

A lone traveler could be seen cresting a rise far north of their position. His form shivered on the horizon, like the ripple of a stone dropped into water. He carried no wares and drove no livestock, but from the great distance no other feature could be distinguished. The traveler hung for a moment on the rib, and then disappeared into the rocks below. It was not until the traveler unexpectedly rounded a corner of the trail less than a hundred paces before them that they were able to fully assess his appearance.

The man was strikingly tall, at least a head above Micah. He supported wide shoulders and a thick torso. His beard was matted and long, untamed save for an ornate braid in the center. The hair on his head hung low in earthy locks. It curled into the fur of his coat where the hairs of animal and man were indistinguishable. He gripped a thick wooden staff in one hand. But it was not the man's stature or his unruly state that caught both Micah and Zachary so unexpectedly, it was the man's skin. His body was painted blue. It was the same blue of the morning sky, of the river of the valley, and of the deep ice that broke on the skulls of The Divide. And out of the blue his eyes floated like white clouds over the heavens.

Neither Zachary nor Micah spoke as the man approached them, but his eyes did not linger upon them. Indeed, they seemed to flit and wander through Micah and Zachary, as if they were but water. The man moved at such speed that he had walked between them before Zachary found his voice.

"Have you come from the place of the White Mountain?"

The man stopped as if Zachary had tightened a chain about his neck. He did not turn, but from under his great cloak of furs his back swelled with mountain air, and as he spoke the air escaped him like bellows.

"From above its beating heart I walk."

Zachary glanced at Micah with a mix of confusion and hope. "And how far is it that you have walked from that place?"

"By the gods, though I may walk far, my soul remains." The man's voice was the wind, a passing chill.

"I'm not sure that you understand me," Zachary said with uncertainty. "How many days walk to the White Mountain?"

"I plead to thee, do not be angry with my wandering."

"There is no need to plead, but do tell me, are you far from the Mountain?"

The man's hands curled into fists, and his body began to shake. "Do not listen to him, I am lost and cannot see!" His steady breathing now came at sharp bursts, and suddenly he whirled to face Zachary. His mouth sagged open in despair and from his throat the wind began to howl. The man fell to his knees, and his hands rose to claw desperately at his white and bloodless eyes. It was but paint and not his eyes that were as white as the clouds, for his eyes were shut by the swollen folds of his skin at which he pried at with his fingernails.

Startled, Zachary stepped back from the man who groped in the dirt. "Gods be merciful, what has happened to you?"

"The gods are merciful!" the man screamed. "The gods spared me, a wretch and a demon! I do not deserve sight; I did not deserve to see! The White Mountain chooses the blessed, and I am not among them." He gripped his chest with a blue hand. "There is blackness in my heart. Hear me, traveler! I make my case before the gods! I am blemished, I have not a heart of snow. I do not deserve to be blessed." The man broke into sobs. His eyes dripped tears from the folds, and his face contorted with pain.

"This was done to you, by the gods? By the White Mountain?" Micah's voice was strangled with fear.

The man clenched a callous fist and thrust it with anger into the soil. "Do you not hear me? The gods are merciful, for I deserve death. The gods be praised! Your servant will return!" He brought his hands back to his face and wept bitterly.

"Do you-," Zachary stammered, "Do you hail from the monastery below the Mountain?" Micah shot him a quizzical look, but Zachary ignored it. The man said nothing but continued to weep. "And you sought to climb the White Mountain, to earn its blessing?"

"Oh the gods, I must bear the burden of evil on my forehead, for all could see it but my own eyes! No, it is good that I am laid bare, the gods can see my suffering. If only I had eyes to see, I should give my heart to see where I have left my soul!" The man lifted his face from the dust of the trail. His hair hung in tangles, but they could not hide the piercing white façade of his painted eyes. He tilted his head back, and for a moment the break of a smile washed over his lips. "There it stands," he sighed, his voice again the gentle wind of the valley. "With shoulders as wide as The Divide, and a body that ever glitters white with snow. A Child of the World, beloved by the gods. A gift, so that we too may see. Can you see it, traveler?" His raised a blue stained finger to the north, pointed high into the heavens.

Micah turned, but he only saw a towering cloud to the north that threatened itself over the valley. "There is nothing, poor man! You have not eyes to see; you must be farther than you realize. Come Zachary, do we have any provisions we can share?" He looked to Zachary, but Zachary did not return his gaze. Instead, Zachary was fixed on the great cloud to the north. And in his features Micah saw the faces of those who had passed them travelling south on the ancient trail. He saw Zachary's face split with disbelief, melt into wonder, and shake into a trembling fear. Micah turned to face the north once more.

The cloud hung over the valley. It severed the sky into two halves, one of white and one of clear blue. Micah studied the seam. It was impossibly sharp, and unlike any cloud he had ever seen. It was a tremendous wedge, pyramidal, an obelisk. It ran into a narrow point that soared high above even the boldest Knight of the Hall. And then Micah saw. He doubted his eyes, he doubted his mind, but he could not doubt his soul. It bellowed from the pits of his being; it screamed and pulled and thrashed against its chains. It begged him not to turn from the north, for before him, above him, and beyond him, the White Mountain sat on its throne. The Lord of the Hall, King of The Divide, holiest of summits. It shattered the sky, for it was the sky over them. A temple of snow, wider than the valley that could hold it.

"Can you doubt its purpose?" The man spoke with tears in his beard. "Can you doubt its purity? Traveler, what is it like? Does the wanton cloud dare to break on its shoulders? Does the high wind still blow?"

From over the eastern ridge a shimmering trail of white departed the mountain. It was lost into the chest of a nearby cloud that moved quickly below the crest of the White Mountain, below the summit which did not hide but stood proudly illuminated by the light of the sun. Micah's eyes could not leave the summit, for it beckoned to him unlike any call he had felt before. His blood coursed with courage and fear, with passionate love and a boiling hatred. His soul had broken its bonds, it had risen from his chest, and it threatened to leap from his open mouth.

"It cannot be doubted," Zachary muttered aloud. "For it has touched heaven."

"No traveler, none can touch heaven, not even the White Mountain. It is a blessing, a gift to the mortal! A gift won by ascension alone." The man no longer wept. His face was drawn tightly; the blue ran down his cheeks in swirling streaks. "I will return; by the gods I will return when at last I am forgiven." The man rose from the trail. He said nothing, but faced south, away from Micah and Zachary. His broad shoulders rose and fell. "Traveler, look upon me no more. Forget my passing, for it is but a gust within these canyon walls." Without another word, the man left them.

"Zachary," Micah said, tearing his eyes from the White Mountain to watch the man depart. "What monastery do you speak of? Could such a man be a monk of any order?"

Zachary shook his head. "Of the White Mountain, I was sure. But the monks of the mountain are legend to my people. They are said to be the mightiest of climbers, and yet they climb nothing but the White Mountain. When the weather is warm, when the snow is stable, only then do they seek out its blessing. They are said to live high on its slopes, in a temple of stone. I thought it a good tale, until I saw one today."

"But what of him? He was not a man blessed, but cursed!"

"Perhaps his purpose was not just." Zachary was again lost in the slopes of the mountain. "Our purpose is just, is it not? Surely we shall find favor with heaven."

Micah did not answer, but set his jaw firmly. The White Mountain repeated its call, and his skin crawled. At last, he spoke. "Your purpose is just; you shall find favor."

Zachary found himself, and offered an encouraging, crooked smile. "Not just I, dear friend. Together, we shall find favor! And the gods will share the answers to our souls, I know it! This is surely the sight the blind monk spoke of."

"My friend, I hope that you are right."

PRIDE

The seeker is but a novice to love, for he has spent his life in the wilderness. As a child he was curious, for he had wonder. As a youth he was determined, for he had powerful desire. As a man he feels love, for his passion points to purpose. But the seeker has not yet found his purpose, though he feels its tender touch. He closes his eyes in a room of vibrant colors, refuses to smell when the plate is passed before him, and screams when he hears a whisper. He maintains that purpose is his own blade to wield.

In the following day, the flowing river ended. It had weakened as they passed each Knight's offering, until its source finally ran gurgling from beneath a tremendous wall of ice. The headwaters of the Hall were numbing to the touch, and with each swallow left the mouth steaming and red. Micah kept his water skin beneath his coat and close to his skin so that it would not freeze, though it chilled him to do so.

Micah and Zachary followed the trail as it circumnavigated the wall of ice to the west. It followed a notch in the valley side that was dry and allowed access over the wall. The trail stayed high on the western edge, dodging through tall rocks but following well-trodden earth. Micah and Zachary were grateful, for the wall that devoured the headwaters splintered into a menagerie of broken ice. It was a stagnant river of frost that fractured under the rising sun. It was pierced with lucid blue irises whose groaning black pupils followed their steps; it split with gaping wounds that spanned its entire breadth, a white trunk cut carelessly by the lumberjack's blow. To the north it ran, filling the valley with its girth until it met the King of the Hall. The White Mountain nourished the stagnant flow from the hem of its snowy coat.

The White Mountain was close now. No Knight obstructed its King, no subordinate grew from its shoulders. The gutter of ice that ushered mortals into the valley could be directly traced from the headwaters to the mountain's throne.

But as the White Mountain loomed ever closer, its high summit retreated until it could no longer be discerned among the billowing false summits of snow. And yet, its call could still be heard, faint amongst the dull beating of Micah's heart.

They walked the old trail to its junction, to the terminus by which all travelers of the Northern Divide find their end. There sprouted a small settlement, inhabited by a lonely few who fed on the riches of distant nations. It was a hub of commerce, surviving by the backs of those who desired trade across The Divide but did not dare to cross it; to occupy such a land required hard skin and sleepless nights. It was erected of stone, hide and ice. As Micah passed each tenant he saw the alpine chisel on their bodies. He watched with wonder as they handled their goods, indifferent to the forces of The Divide. Those foreign to the land struggled to barter in the blowing gale while the natives simply blinked away any accumulation of frost. Micah personally found that his will to strike fair trade dwindled with every moment a shopkeeper let him stand haggling in the cold.

As the sun descended to the west, Micah and Zachary had managed to trade their last valuables for suitable clothing, ample supplies, and a shelter for the night. The light faded quickly, and although the village was blanketed in darkness, the White Mountain bloomed as a torch late into the evening. The cold could not force them into their shelter until the last rays left the crown of the King, after which they huddled gratefully within its blanketed walls. There was no light in the tent, no sound save for their sharp, uneven breath.

"Micah, can you sleep in this cold?" Zachary shuffled in the darkness.

"No, but I'm afraid that it is not the cold that is preventing me."

Zachary was quiet. Visions of the White Mountain still lingered in their minds.

"I met a man on the trail, Micah, before we crossed paths. He was old and broken and wore a face cut from stone. I had forgotten him until I saw the others in this village, for they wear the same face."

Micah listened from within the seal of blankets pulled tightly over his head. Zachary paused for an answer, but accepted his silence. "He spoke to me when my companions were away, hunting. They never saw his face. Do you know what he said to me? He told me a story Micah, a story that makes me bleed with fear before the White Mountain. Can I tell it to you, so that you may help me to understand it?"

"Of course, Zachary."

"Thank you, my friend." He tried to take a long breath, but was caught in a fit of coughing. When it subsided, Zachary spoke.

"The story he told went like this, as I best remember it: there once was a great climber of the south; one who did not fear the mountains, for his strength surpassed even their jealousy. He was a man fashioned after the gods themselves, and he held no other purpose than to share in their magnificence. And so he climbed each peak, the next always higher than the first.

"But one day the man stood on the highest peak of the Southern Range, and looking around saw that there was none higher. And so he waited for joy, for he felt that surely it was his due. The man waited on the summit for a day and a night, but his heart was silent. So he waited again for a day and a night, and still the gods did not bless him. He waited a third day, and as the evening fell the gods punished him greatly. He was cast down from the summit in disgrace.

"The great climber wept for his spirit, but through his tears he saw the mighty slopes and thought to himself, 'Surely there is no joy on the summit, but is it not great indeed to ascend? To put each foot above the last, to see the heavens fast approaching? For only there my soul has felt the touch of joy.' So the great climber ascended each peak of the south, this time starting in the lowest valley and reaching the highest peak. His strength was unmatched, his courage unbounded. He climbed in snow, he climbed in rain. He dodged the dogs of hell and even felt their lash upon his back.

"There came a day when the man ascended the tallest ridge of the most prominent spire of the range, and as he climbed he listened closely for the joy in his heart. He felt the warmth of its presence, but when he crested the spire it dropped away like a stone. The man looked out in the mighty range and saw that there was none other as great as he, and that there was no route like that which he had ascended. And he waited not one, not two, but three days atop the tall spire before he was again cruelly punished by the gods. They beat his face with wind, they broke his body with stone, and they left him within a hairs breadth from the end of his life.

"The great climber was humbled by the gods, and in his despair he begged to know how he could find his joy, how he could satisfy the hunger of his immortal soul. 'Surely there is no joy on the summit, and every climb must reach an end. What then can my mortal body do? How can I satisfy my thirst? If it is not the climb, nor the summit, then why does my soul drive me to ascend the high peaks?' The great climber heard no answer, and was filled with rage. He looked up at the Southern Range, at the most dangerous and terrible of routes and said, 'Must I die to find my joy? I am the strongest of men, my courage is unbounded, but the gods can break me. By the gods I will climb once more, to find my joy, for there is no other route that is more terrible than this.'

"And so he climbed alone on the east buttress of the Goblin's Tower, a spire of vertical rock and of frozen snow. As he climbed the gods sent hail and wind to cast him from his purchase. The great climber felt fear for the first time, but he continued to climb. He did not slip, he did not falter, and he reached the summit triumphant.

"Alone, cold, afraid, the great climber waited. He waited for three days, but the joy he desired never came. On the third day he descended, not cast out by the gods but by his own will. He spent many days in the valleys, and his heart darkened. 'The gods deny me joy, though they gave me my soul to pursue it. Is this prize not worthy of it? I have seen joy in men who have accomplished far less than I, the strongest of climbers! Is it then unworthy of my strength?' The great climber pulled his hair in anguish, but his soul remained hungry. So the great climber left the south to find a worthy challenge, one that would earn his right to joy. He travels the land eternally, always hungry, never satisfied. He has no equal. He has no joy. That is the burden of the great climber."

Zachary ended the tale with a heavy cough. Micah had since peeled back the layers of fur that sheltered him from the cold so that he could better listen. He sat up, listening to his friend stifle his fit in the darkness.

"It is but a tale, one that I have heard some form of before."

"The climber," Zachary regained control of his breath, "The old man told me his name. Micah, his name was Giralt."

"Giralt, the very man who summited the Twisted Peak, who passed through the valley of my home? Impossible!"

"I thought the same. But Micah, say that it is true, what does it mean? If he could not find the truth, then how could we? We, who are not great, we who are not seasoned climbers!"

"It cannot be true!" Micah bit back fiercely. "If Giralt did seek out the greatest of peaks, surely he too would incur the blessing of the White Mountain! He too would be blessed; he too would share in its purpose!"

"But if the story is true," Zachary stammered, "What are we doing here, at the base of the King of The Divide, where we have no hope to succeed, and like Giralt, no hope for answers? Micah, when I first laid eyes on the White Mountain I knew that it was too great, too holy, that we would surely perish on its slopes! And if its promise is not joy, if its promise is not to give us answer to our soul, then why should we try this foolhardy mission? Have you no more love for your life, Micah, or for your family?"

Micah winced as if struck, he bared his teeth and curled his fingers into his blankets. But he stayed his tongue, and after his anger subsided he felt the old thorn of regret that had been left lodged into his heart. "Of course I love my family." He sat with hunched shoulders, feeling the weight of his words. "But can you not feel it Zachary? Can you not feel the call? It pierces my skin, overcomes my mind, and sings to my very soul! Oh, to hear again the chorus of song as I climbed the Twisted Peak, I would happily give my life!" He squared his shoulders, and grimaced. "If I must, I will give my life, for

100

it is better to taste that joy then to live forever without it. Giralt may not have found his joy, but I know why he climbs. I feel why he climbs, and it is why I must ascend the White Mountain. You said yourself that the song cannot be wicked, that it must be a sign of something holy. I believe you now Zachary. Do you still doubt me?"

The tent was silent save for Micah's now ragged breath. It flared with fire and burned his chest despite the cold. "I believe you," Zachary answered in the dark. "I believe you not by your words but by your passion. I long to feel what you have on the back of the Twisted Peak. I will not lose this chance to do so."

"I am glad," Micah said, slouching back into his bed. "We have plenty of provisions, and I have no desire to stay in this cold place for long. We should start for the White Mountain tomorrow, and make camp on its flanks."

"As you say," Zachary answered. He remained seated for some time before finally slipping into his bed for warmth. "It will be a great adventure, Micah. One that I shall always remember."

"As shall I," Micah murmured sleepily. But his eyes were open wide.

COURTSHIP

Passion and purpose, these are the seeds of love. A seeker listens to his heart, but to love he must marry heart and mind. For the heart must inspire the mind, and the mind guides the heart. To what end is this union upheld? The seeker is weary, for long has he obeyed his reckless desire. To one such as him the menagerie of purpose is of minor consequence to love. In the presence of many such beauties, the choice seems to be simple. This is the hubris of the seeker, for he is therefore still a slave to desire.

The sun had not yet touched the summit of the White Mountain when Zachary and Micah emerged from their shelter, but the sky was a gradient of blues. They assembled their packs in silence, busying themselves with trivialities despite the morning chill. They cast furtive glances to the north, but never let it occupy their vision for long. After a prolonged meal in which both members ate little, they left the site for the White Mountain.

No longer did they walk the marked paths of The Divide. Though they had not yet encountered any snow, the terrain was rough, uneven, and tedious work. The ground was littered with small rocks that had been lodged into the eddy currents of the frozen runoff that flowed from the mountain. To avoid slipping they stepped carefully from stone to stone. Both were grateful for their current choice of route, however, as the vast river of ice yawned its many blue mouths and waited patiently beside them.

The valley did not rise sharply, and as such Micah and Zachary made a quick approach to the base of the mountain. The sun had since risen, and they decided to stop and better assess their options on the southern face. The White Mountain rolled overhead, a blanket of blinding white in the afternoon sun. They craned their necks back, squinted, and shielded their eyes between fingers, and were able to discern a few features in the snow.

The great river of ice rose with the side of the mountain, and soared high on its face. It was even more fractured on the incline, the sheets of ice separated and toppled over one another. Neither Zachary nor Micah were eager to navigate such treacherous terrain, and so they decided to push for the western ridge where the travel would hopefully be more uniform. They rose, gripped their packs, and began to move once more.

Micah's first steps on the mountain brought him protest from his body; his bones ached and his joints creaked with each footfall. His breath, which had grown shorter each day as they had approached the White Mountain, felt thinner still. His body sweat profusely under his furs, but once exposed was immediately chilled by the lick of powdered snow. The ground now carried a light dusting of snow through which Micah could not identify patches of ice, causing him to dance on the rocks. His mind struggled to conjure how the travel would change when they reached the higher snowpack; he knew that it could only deepen.

But when Micah and Zachary stopped to rest after the sun had travelled a hands breadth in the sky, Micah found himself painted with a ridiculous smile. He did not know he wore it until his mind relaxed from the toil of travel. He removed the gloves on his hands and touched his face in wonder.

"I am hot, I have a headache, my mouth is dry and my feet dislike these boots," Zachary's voice rang out from beside Micah. He turned, and saw that Zachary wore the same giddy smile as he. "But I would not be anywhere else." He nodded to the south.

The Hall of the White Mountain was laid out before them, and they sat at the steps of its throne. Cut by the crescent moon laid to rest it carved a channel to the south; the river emerging from the thicket of ice now many leagues away and a thousand paces below. And the tall Knights stood on either side, looking upon the face of their king for grace, for guidance, and for purpose. They rose still above the perch of Micah and Zachary, proudly donning their helms of ice and

103

puffing breastplates of unblemished white stone. They watched as two mortals climbed to meet their king.

"It's beautiful," Micah said simply. "I could not see it from below."

"I saw it, but it was a mere glimpse compared to this. Micah, though my body suffers, my spirit soars! Is this what it means to ascend? Is this why you climb?"

"This is but a taste," Micah grinned. "Do you feel rested Zachary? We have a long way to climb still before nightfall."

"No," Zachary replied, "But let us continue, I burn to move my legs again!"

They climbed until the sun began to dip below the horizon, and its golden rays were swept to the summit by a wave of shadow. Micah and Zachary stopped and constructed a shelter of tarpaulin and staked it firmly to the cold soil. They sat inside and ate with renewed appetite. They held the canvas' flap open and watched as darkness flooded the Hall. The horizon to the south glowed well after the land had disappeared save for a few yellow flames that dotted the junction town below.

The following morning, they awoke to an unblemished sky of faded blue. The air frosted about their mouths, and the sun had not yet touched their encampment. To stave off the cold which had awoken them, Micah and Zachary threw on their remaining layers and broke camp after a small meal. The soil crunched beneath their feet as they worked.

They were silent as the previous morning, but this time the silence was met by their grinning faces and eager hands. They indulged in the southern face of the White Mountain, drinking in its features. From their new vantage they could see that to gain the west ridge they would need to ascend a glossy chute of snow that ran between the cliff bands that guarded the ridge. They left their camp in high spirits.

As Micah and Zachary climbed to the chute, the snow on the ground began to accumulate. Soon their boots no longer touched the soil. The snow was firm however, and by kicking steps they could make slow progress on the incline which seemed to grow with every step. They became lost on the white face, entrenched in the task of simply placing each foot above the next. Neither preferred to look above them, for their progress had become so slow that the chute seemed only to recede as the sun crawled across the sky. The white face upon which they clung had expanded to encompass the entirety of their view.

Though the climbing was difficult, both Zachary and Micah together began the climb in good spirits, encouraging one another to continue up the face. But each man fought his own internal battle when the other was not looking. As Micah pushed into the snow he first feared for his warmth, but soon found that his face and body burned with the heat of the sun. He removed most of his layers, but then the sun relentlessly stung at his skin. He was careful to protect his body from direct light, though it caused him to sweat excessively. And when the sun had risen to its apex in the sky, Micah found that the snow itself was lit like a fire, and that his eyes ached under its white glare. He squinted through closed fingers, and finally resolved to shut his eyes and climb by feel, for the terrain was monotone and did not require sight.

The chute that had appeared so far from them suddenly sprung forward, and it was unexpected when they found themselves at its mouth. It was wide at its base, but narrowed to only a few shoulders width at its neck. The cliffs on either side loomed overhead and bore slender fangs of ice that ran with water under the afternoon sun. The chute ran steep; it left the field of snow abruptly and soared to the seat of the west ridge.

The surrounding rock wore a coat of snow that hid a thick slab of ice underneath, providing no traction with the leather of their boots. Micah and Zachary felt the snow at the base of the chute, and found that their feet sunk well into its back. Sharing uneasy smiles, they started to climb. Micah led at first, but soon grew weary from digging his way into the snow to find suitable purchase. They began to switch leads, neither lasting long under the conditions. The snow was wet and slid easily. They found that no step held under their full weight, and were forced to balance between movements to maintain a delicate ascent.

Zachary was in the lead when they reached the neck of the chute. It was impossibly lofted, steeper than even the preceding slope. Zachary pushed desperately into its soft face, raining debris down on Micah's head. Micah, for fear of sliding down the chute, did not dare take cover, but instead took the assault with a bent forehead and shivering skin.

"Micah!" Zachary called out from above. "There is nothing to take hold of; it cannot be ascended!" A crack of desperation broke in his voice.

Micah chanced a glance through the tumble of snow at his partner. Zachary was sunk to his hips and right shoulder in the neck of snow. The rock hedged them in on either side; there was scarcely room for two men at its constriction. The snow above clogged the chokepoint, and Zachary had been prying away its layers to no avail.

"We must go back down! There must be another-," but Zachary did not finish his sentence, for at that moment they heard the ice overhead splinter and with a heavy sigh the choke of snow slipped from the mountainside. Zachary immediately vanished into its mass, and though Micah braced himself into the snow he too was swallowed. The tumble struck him hard, and in the whirlwind of whites and blues Micah lost consciousness.

PAIN

The seeker has felt suffering, he has been hurt by failure and by the pursuit. But the seeker feels only passion, and in passion can only bleed so much. But the lover, he feels a pain unlike any other. For though his love may hurt him, he cannot refuse it. He cannot deny it; he cannot fight it. He must accept it, and embrace it. For if he does truly love it, to destroy a part of the whole would be to no longer love. The pain, the joy, are they not inseparable?

There was no wind on the mountain, and no sound could penetrate the air. It was frozen like the water on the rocks, like the snow that corniced over the cliffs and the blue sky above. The mountain spoke very little, for even a whisper meant death. Indeed, life was permitted by its grace alone.

Micah awoke by the rasp of his own slow breathing. His chest was heavy and damp. His eyes rolled open, and the sun blinded them. He felt his arm twitch, and then his legs, though his legs were stiff. Micah looked down at his legs. He could not see them; they were not beneath him. He only saw white as brilliant as the sun that blinded him from above.

He groaned as the blood began to beat back into his body. With his free arm, he tried to push away the snow that was locked in around his chest. It was still wet, and though heavy he was able to free his torso. His legs soon followed, and he was free.

Micah looked around. He sat at the base of the chute amidst a rubble of loose snow that rested in chunks. They left little trails that ran up the face of the chute and into its neck. Blinking back his spinning head, he stumbled to his feet.

"Zachary!" he shouted, scouring the chute for an indication of his companion.

"I am here," he heard from behind him. Micah spun, and saw that his friend lay partially under the same path of debris that he had not ten paces below him.

"Are you hurt?" Micah stammered as he made uneasy steps down the slope.

"I do not know," Zachary admitted. With effort he pushed the snow from his body, and gathered himself into a sitting position. Micah stumbled to his side and fell into the snow beside him. His body had begun to protest; from his head to his toes it ached dully.

Zachary probed his body for injury, and seemed satisfied. "I hurt, but I am not injured. You seem to be walking, at least."

Micah did not answer, but let his head fall back into the snow. Zachary watched him, and then turned to the chute. They sat in a stupor as their heads gradually cleared, though in the heat of the day there remained a throbbing pain at their temples. Neither felt the strength to speak, and with blankets to protect their skin both eventually fell asleep sprawled on the snow. It was a broken sleep, disturbed by sweat on their face and ice under their backs. They rested until the sun had begun to retreat below the horizon, and the temperature dropped. Easing themselves from the snow, they managed to find a rocky outcrop beneath the cliff band that offered shelter from wind and enough soil to sleep on. They pitched a rough camp, and settled in for the night.

"That was foolish; I could have killed us both. By the grace of the gods we breathe still." The light was dim on the tarpaulin, and Zachary's face was a ghostly silhouette against its glow. He was still, watching the Hall fade away through a seam in the canvas.

"By their grace? Or by their jealousy did we fall?" Micah propped his head up on his pack. He spoke through his teeth. "Tell me Zachary, do you still ascend for so noble a goal?"

Zachary thought for a moment. "Perhaps my heart did betray me. But as I sit, my soul seeks nothing but answers, Micah, as it always has. What do you seek?"

"I follow my soul, though I do not know where it leads me. There is something for me on top of this mountain, I feel it in my bones, and I taste it in the air. Zachary, I will climb this mountain with or without blessing. For it has been placed inside me to ascend this mountain, by none other than the gods."

"Are you not afraid? Afraid to die, so very far from home?"

"You know that I am afraid. I am terrified, because when I look up at the White Mountain I hear its call. I am terrified because I cannot ignore it. Even when I am cast down, I wish to return. I cannot explain it, Zachary- it confounds my senses, and it defies my very reason! Why should I desire something bent on destroying me, why do I revel in its misery, why am I unsatisfied watching from the valley below? If only, Zachary, I could be at peace with such a life- I could look upon the White Mountain and enjoy its beauty from afar!"

"Could you? Could you ever look upon the White Mountain and see its beauty from below? Micah, as a man who lived on the doorstep of The Divide, I believed that I understood its anger, its suffering, and its beauty. But to see it from this vantage, I now see that I was blind. Do you know why, Micah? Do you know why I did not love the mountains as I do now?"

"No, Zachary. I do not know why."

"I believe that it is because I never sank my legs into the freezing snow. I never felt the bitter wind across my cheeks. I never surrendered my life into their hands, for that is what we have done now, Micah. It is by their grace that we will summit. A twitch on their backs, a shallow breath of their air, and we are forever lost. Can you not sense it?"

"I can."

"And tell me Micah, and do be honest with yourself. Would you climb them if it were any other way?"

"No," Micah said.

"Why is it then; that which terrifies us most has stolen our hearts?" The dawn light had faded, and Zachary was consumed by darkness. "That is why I climb with you now. I wish to know this answer."

"Perhaps at the summit, you will have your answer," Micah muttered.

"Perhaps," Zachary answered, a spark of hope in his voice. "I do not expect it to be easy, nor would I wish it to be so." His figure turned in the falling light, facing Micah. "But we were nearly lost today, never to climb again. I am not deaf to warning, and if the gods should continue to reject my passage, I would descend with humility."

"Then you shall descend alone."

"But can you not see such futility? By the grace of the gods you are permitted to summit, by their will alone may you receive such a blessing. You entered a land where you no longer have power, where each moment can steal your life away. Do not be so bold as to assume you can overcome this obstacle alone!"

"If the gods have placed such a wretched soul inside me, then who am I to deny it? I will climb by faith, and should the gods be cruel enough to strike me down, then so be it."

Micah's tone adopted a harsh note of finality, and sensing it Zachary did not reply, but pulled his sheets over his body, and tried to sleep.

ALLURE

The seeker is poor in purpose, and so his love is blind. Perhaps his bride does stand before him: he does not know it. He does not see its beauty; his admiration is unfounded, ugly. He sees a silhouette, a flash of light, an enticing scent but no more. How can he see what is beautiful if he does not understand its purpose? How can he love if he does not know his purpose? For it is an intersection of passion and purpose, to love. To his vacant eyes, this design is utterly lost. And so even the allure of his true bride may forsake him.

The White Mountain shined in the moonlight, a mountain amid mountains, a King amongst Kings, the holiest subject of the divine. But late into the night, The Divide gathered its breath, and blew a tremendous gale from the east. It collected the clouds of nearby valleys and rolled them up and over the broad shoulders of the Mountain. They twisted and whirled over its high ramparts, breaking over the east ridge and casting themselves like white ocean spray far over the southern face. As the sun threatened dawn, The Divide blew a mighty breath and the waves crested the ridge. They splashed down over the river of ice below, flooding the Hall, swallowing the settlement below. The red light of dawn flickered over the ridge as the ocean of cloud rippled over the ridgeline. It seethed in the unceasing breath of The Divide.

The tarpaulin flapped erratically throughout the night. Micah and Zachary did not sleep, but spent most hours watching their hasty staking and mending their shelter when the wind proved too great. When dawn came they were eager to leave their shelter and stretch cold fingers in the sun, but found that the east wind left them cradling freezing digits. They managed to pack their shelter without sacrificing it to the wind, and watched impatiently for the light to soften the snow. The snow was firm, frozen into a sheet by the evening air, and neither Micah nor Zachary could kick easy steps.

They did not wait for long, as their bodies were left unsheltered in the wind they felt their bare skin burn and their lips chap. It was a decision of little deliberation when they decided to ascend despite the hardened snowpack. As they climbed, the snow made them slip, the wind forced them to crouch and the cold tightened their movements. When the sun finally touched them directly, they were able to peek out from the mental cocoons they had spun in order to reach it.

Neither felt that the chute or any of its neighboring cousins were safe for travel after their accident, and so they resolved to move east along the bottom of the cliff band. They soon found this too proved dangerous, as frequent snaps announced the release of rocks from above. This pressured them downhill, where the rock fall could at least be first identified and then avoided. Discouraged, they pressed on, the gale persisting throughout the morning.

Micah became dimly aware from within the confines of his thick hood that the flow of ice was fast approaching. He kept an eye on the slopes above them, but could not find a suitable avenue to escape to the southwest ridge. But as the flow drew closer, he began to reconsider their decision to forgo the chute. The ice was more fractured than he had anticipated; it was ravaged by the gaping blue seams. There seemed no conceivable route through the fractures, and yet their alternative was to ascend a wall of vertical stone.

The wind howled in Micah's ears. It pushed on his face, it tried to turn his body from the east to which he was bent. He plodded each foot before the last, making little calculation in doing so such that he could abandon reality and recede into a safer place. He walked through tall blades of grass; they tickled the hair on his legs as he passed. The sun warmed his body against a light prevailing breeze, and the sound of bells floated on the air. He stopped. All was a sea of yellow, with a jagged edge of white on the horizon that sliced into a parallel surface of blue. The smell of grass and blossoms kissed his nose, and he felt his heart settle into an easy rhythm. But his feet, they were cold. He wiggled his toes, each one at a time, but they cried out against him. Micah tore his eyes from the white jagged line, and he looked down.

112

He saw his feet bundled in leather that had grown a wreath of frost at the tips. He saw the white snow run over them, and a bridge of translucent ice tucked underneath. And then he looked beyond it into the arterial vein of the Mountain. Blackness, lipped in deep marbled blue, so deep that even the light of the sun could not penetrate, pulsating with the beating heart of the White Mountain. The thin plane of ice that supported him creaked unhappily. Gently, and without breath, he stepped across and onto firm snow.

Zachary did not follow, but instead circumnavigated the seam to join Micah. They did not dare approach its mouth, and in a state of terror critically examined every subsequent footstep. They decided to cease their traverse, and to ascend again, skirting the edge of the flow in hopes to avoid more fissures. The river of ice was far wider than they anticipated, with gaping cracks reaching out beyond its shores, craftily hidden beneath a thin dusting of snow and ice. But the cliffs ran flush with the ice flow above them; to gain it they would be forced to take the river's edge.

So Micah and Zachary bent their bodies north once more. The snow had blown into a thin crust which their feet easily punched through, and it provided them with sufficient traction, though it made lifting each foot above the snow impractical. Instead they punched steps through the surface crust with their clenched fists, and waded each foot into its proper seating through the softer layer beneath. The sun now hung high in the sky, and the snow scorched their eyes. They struggled to see, but refused to fully shelter their eyes lest the Mountain swallow them whole.

Wind screamed along the shell of frozen snow. It carried a light dusting of powder that bounced and abraded ice, rock, and flesh. Micah felt its sting across his nose, though he pulled his head back deep within his hood. He felt it bite at his wrists and at his lower back as his jacket shuffled during each step, exposing small sections of his body in turn. His body, his skin, ran cold as the crust of the White Mountain. The cold seeped into his blood, and threatened to snuff the weak flame alight within his chest.

They encountered more cracks in the mountainside, but none that could halt their advance. Though it required several agonizing hours, they managed to pick their way up along the edge of the ice fall and above the cliffs. They rested briefly at this new vantage, but could find no reprieve from the gale. After a short spell of shivering in the open snow, they turned north once more.

Micah's mind spun in dizzying circles about the miserable state; it had become a sickening cavity for his suffering. The bite of wind on his cheeks, the glare of the snow, the chill on his limbs- all could be contended with individually, but united were indomitable. He could not escape his discomfort, though he tried desperately. He squinted through the white blaze, and was conscious of every step he took. Although his mind held no rationale for his climb, his soul still sung the melody of the White Mountain to his beating heart, and his legs continued to follow its cadence.

They had been climbing for the better half of the day, but the white face still hid its summit from view. Micah halted to examine the route above, but found that he could not recognize any feature, and so held no distinct idea of their position. With a frown, he shook back the protest of his mind and resumed his step. But a strained shout behind him caused him to stop.

"Please, wait! The snow- my eyes," Zachary's voice fluttered on the wind. Micah, turning slowly, cracked open one eye down the slope. Zachary swayed below him, buffeted with each gust and no longer climbing, standing with his bare hands searching across his face.

"Zachary," Micah murmured, and then remembering the gale began to shout. "Zachary! What is wrong? Why have you stopped?"

Zachary pulled his hands from his face, and watched them with wide eyes. He blinked repeatedly, intentionally, but his expression grew only more desperate. "Micah!" He turned his gaze uphill. "The snow Micah, it is too bright!"

Despite himself Micah felt a flare of irritation, but still made clumsy steps back down to his partner's side. Zachary still held his wriggling fingers in the wind.

"I thought it just a headache, but my eyes, they grew sore, and now Micah, my very hands before me appear soft, like the fur of a coat!" He looked at Micah blankly. "Though you stand before me, you are not as I have seen before; I can hardly make sense of you from the snow!"

Micah fidgeted in the wind, struggling to catch Zachary's words over the gale. "Zachary, I too am in pain, but we cannot stop now while there is daylight left!"

"It is not just pain, but my sight!" Zachary dropped his eyes to the ground, and his mouth fell open. "The snow, Micah! I have not closed my eyes, for I was afraid to be taken by the Mountain! But the snow, it is like the sun!"

Micah lifted his eyes, and studied Zachary's. They were streaked with red, and the lids had begun to swell. "Then shelter them, Zachary. Use a cloth, block them from the snow, they will mend!" He offered a strained smile as Zachary stooped to pull a wool sock from his pack. Zachary drew it across his eyes, and tied it as a blindfold.

"Still I will not be able to see; we should make shelter here, until I am healed!"

The wind surged suddenly, and both Micah and Zachary were forced to their knees. Micah strained to shout over its scream, "We cannot stay here; there is no shelter from this wind!"

Zachary tucked his hands beneath his coat, and shook his head violently. "Then we dig in the snow; there is no way for me to travel!"

"No Zachary, not while there is still time yet to climb! Do you not wish to stand on the summit? Do you not wish to have your questions answered? Do not let this stop you from ascension!"

"Micah! I am blinded, what if I am to misstep on the mountain?"

"Let me guide you, Zachary! Follow me to the summit; our purpose is holy; we shall not be denied our blessing!"

"Micah," Zachary pleaded. "You do not believe what you say; I know when you are dishonest. Please listen to the Mountain, for it will surely destroy us, but is giving us a final chance to turn away! Are you such a slave, that you cannot deny this chance for another?"

"There will be no other chances!" Micah's body lit with fire, he blazed in the wind and screamed over its howl. "This is it Zachary, there is no greater summit! Why should I turn back now, from the very place that calls to my soul? I told you, it is better to die than to live without joy. I found it once, and already I taste it again!"

"This is no longer joy; this is madness, this is suicide!" Zachary reached a groping hand forward, and caught Micah by the arm. "My friend, I too feel the call of this mountain, I too desire the summit; you know that I wish to satisfy my desire. But this," he swept his free hand around him. "This is not the way! The gods have shown us, and it is as the monk says, they are merciful! But you would be a fool to ignore these warnings, and you would be a fool to prize this mountain over your life, and your soul!"

"This mountain already carries my soul, it has been forcibly taken from me, and it is by the summit alone that I may find it again!" The Divide blew its mightiest breath, and again Micah and Zachary were cast into the snow. Micah pushed himself to his feet, and stood over Zachary. "You cannot understand, you have not climbed before, you do not feel the call as I do. This is my purpose; only by ascension will I ever find peace! Zachary, do you wish to find peace with me?" He bent, and grabbed Zachary by the shoulders. But Zachary yelled in anger, and tore himself from Micah's grasp.

"You have not learned, you will never learn! Go, leave me, find your purpose, and make peace with your soul! I will not blaspheme this mountain anymore; I will not be so proud as to lay claim to a gift of the gods!"

Micah tried once more to take hold of Zachary, but was again pushed aside. "Come with me, Zachary! Do not leave me to do this alone! You know that you must climb!"

"No, Micah! My answers do not require this senselessness; I see it now for what it is, and it is without aim! I have seen the pain of the Mountain, I have seen its beauty, and I can see no more. There is no summit for me, only death. And for you Micah, the gods will find no favor with you! You covet the summit- why should you receive it?" The wind screamed, and Zachary fought to hold the blindfold across his eyes.

"But Zachary, how can you give up the summit, as we have climbed so far to achieve it? You would throw it all away, your chance at peace, your chance for answers, so that you may be safe? To do so is suicide indeed!"

"No, I do not have to climb to find my answers; I do not have to climb to find my purpose. I was a fool to believe in you, I was a fool to follow in your footsteps! You may climb your mountains, but I am returning home." Zachary set his jaw firmly, though his cheek quivered. "Goodbye Micah, I wish that you may find your summit."

"Zachary, do not do this!" Micah's voice choked with tears, and his voice trembled with anguish.

"It is already done."

Micah watched helplessly as Zachary made stumbling footsteps down the White Mountain. He called out to his friend, but received no answer. His mind, his heart, both beseeched him to follow. But his soul, it continued to sing his body north. He stood frozen until Zachary disappeared below the rolling hills of snow.

CLARITY

Is it not the final call of man to love? And yet, how easily love is perverted. In his dying breath the seeker surrenders his love, but for whom does he pledge it? What is deserving of such devotion, of such passion, of such righteous purpose? Is it therefore the final tragedy of the seeker, to gift his heart willingly, to pour out his love, and to witness his bride plunge into it the knife while it is still beating in his open palm? He is destroyed, and as his vision fades he sees the world as it truly was.

Micah bent once more uphill, to the north, to the summit of the White Mountain. The clouds that had swept through the Hall of the Mountain now rose to the sky. They now blew across Micah's body in great wisps, pale and white and icy to the touch. And they began to block the sun, which had already started its descent to the horizon.

A white world ensued, a world that Micah stumbled in, alone, afraid, broken. The gale remained in this existence, a constant reminder that his presence was met with no favor. It now swept down the mountain, tilting his body backwards into the void. But Micah continued to climb.

He could see little, for the snow and sky both cast shades of white that met along a crooked horizon. He could feel little, for as the sun continued to fall the cold began to seep into his body. He could hear little, for the wind roared in his ears. He was consigned to the space of his mind, where he rattled about his senses, unable to escape the veil that had been cast over him. And so he continued to climb, because from within the deep a song was still sung.

The wind howled, shook, and then softened. It held a note, pure in the space around it. And in that emptiness, a distant pulse thrummed. At first it was lost amidst the wind, but gradually it inflated the void. Rhythmically, periodically, it rose into a crescendo that was synchronized with the rapid beating of Micah's heart. He raised his hands to his ears, he screamed into the clouds, but all was lost to the music. And then at once, it stopped.

The sound of soft steps pushing through the snow crept up from below. Micah turned. A dark figure moved in the empty below, a blur of darkness that bobbed silently except for the creak of snow beneath its feet.

"Zachary!" Micah called out. But there was no answer. The figure continued to bob at an even pace, moving with great speed up the Mountain. It grew until Micah could see two legs emerging from a torso, and two arms pumping vigorously.

A man bloomed out of the gray, a man of small stature and of gaunt appearance, supporting a scraggly beard and pebbly eyes. On his back he carried a large rucksack that bulged, but he seemed not to notice its weight. He climbed with even strides, with ease and incredible grace.

The man did not notice Micah, even as he passed him on the Mountain. His dark eyes were locked forward, up the Mountain, on the summit. His face was stretched thin, threatening to split should the man strain himself any further. His mouth hung open and sucked greedy breaths through frosty whiskers. And in a moment Micah saw a deep hunger, a deep longing and terrible suffering. He saw the man's body devour itself to deliver its soul, a soul which kindled a fire that never ceased to consume. A soul that was cursed, destined to climb forever, lost amidst the clouds.

At once Micah's soul ceased its song. He cried out in horror, for the man wore Micah's face.

LOSS

What is the seeker to do, but to retreat? He has given his life for love, but that love was blind. In an instant he is shown his error, and his soul is unhinged. Ever still does it cry for passion, but where there once was an object now is claimed by the void. And so the seeker, the young lover, lies down to bleed.

The lone climber marched towards the summit, and as he moved the wind rushed in to fill his hollowed wake. Its return was violent enough to throw Micah from his stance and headlong into the snow. He broke through the surface and sank into the stiff embrace of the Mountain. The wind tore over his back, inflating his jacket and numbing his skin. It lifted fresh crystals from over the shoulder of the Mountain and with a generous hand dusted Micah's prostrate form. Feeling slipped from his back, his toes, and his face as they were slowly cradled in the many fingers of snow.

The white world before his absent eyes faded to black. His labored breath became slow. At last his soul was quiet, shaking in the recesses of his consciousness. The steady beat of his heart remained the last sensation that stimulated his mind. Gradually, painfully, it emerged from the darkness. It wiggled a timid finger in the snow, twitched a few wet toes in their boot.

Shaking, Micah dug his hands into the Mountain, and rose from his icy shell. As the snow fell from his ears he noticed passively that the wind now only murmured. He felt that the cold was no longer bitter, and gave it no place in his mind. He looked north, to the heavens lost to the clouds. But his soul remained silent, for the face, his face, still burned in his eyes.

He turned, and faced down the Mountain. He dropped his eyes to the snow; his solitary tracks were nearly invisible in the snow.

Suddenly, a name exploded across his mind. "Zachary," he breathed. As he uttered the words his heart burst like the floodwaters of the valley. His legs were reinvigorated, and without a second thought he fled the White Mountain.

The snow continued to fall quietly, and the clouds thickened as he descended. He could see no more than a few faint footsteps before him, but whispered thanks that as much still remained crystalized in the snow. They followed the Mountain down in a jagged fashion, and though he lost the trail several times was able to regain it by simply contouring down the slope. But each time it disappeared he felt his heart freeze in his chest.

He followed them for some time, unable to reconcile the hour of the day, for the cold of the Mountain froze not only water and flesh but the passage of time. He followed them, praying for the second pair of tracks to appear beside his own.

As he plunged each foot into the snow his heart trembled. As time crawled on without mercy he felt his stamina wither. And at the moment he feared he might collapse, his tired eyes stretched in astonishment, for within his tracks another set of boots had clearly occupied. His fears momentarily forgotten, Micah cried out in joy and charged into a clumsy lope down the trail. But his excitement was transitory, for just a hundred paces below his discovery he found that the sets of tracks diverged. An isolated pair began to wander west. Each track was irregularly spaced, and Micah could see many places where their owner had stumbled and fallen.

His heart hushed in his chest. The Mountain shared in its silence, and watched from its perch amidst the heavens, all-knowing but unable to speak. Micah felt its eye upon his guilty head as he followed the tracks in the snow. They left the fresh snow, and encountered a level field of rocks. Here the trail turned in circles, uncertain, weary, dragging in the thin layer of snow. The clouds began to lift, and Micah saw a frozen glove abandoned beside the tracks. The snow was heavily beaten around it, as if its user had spent considerable time searching and finally surrendered.

He continued to follow the tracks. They left the glove, and reluctantly contoured downhill. Micah stopped. The tracks ended abruptly. Before them, the mountain fell away, yielding to the soft echo of the abyss. Micah's heart dared not beat as he recognized the wall that had guarded the southwest ridge open before him. He could see nothing below, only a tongue of ice that streaked vertically across the dripping black rock below into low hanging clouds.

He had no thought as he retraced his steps to the separation of their trails, and resumed his descent at the junction. No fear for life threatened him as he stepped around the dark fissures of the mountain, and in his stupor he reached the bottom of the cliff band quite suddenly. Now safe from the danger of ice, Micah felt a new source of fear begin to prickle across his neck.

The snow continued to fall softly, though the clouds had retreated to the top of the cliff band. Micah's breath escaped him in small puffs, and frost tickled his lips and nose. He moved west along the length of rock, hugging tightly to its junction with the snow. He did not know what it was he searched for, he would not allow his mind to think so far. But he searched the snow all the same.

The air was white, and a fresh sprinkling of frost clung to the rock, riding its many small ledges. There was no sound save for the crunching of Micah's boots. They seemed to hang in the air, echoing throughout the Hall below. And the Hall was flooded white, almost imperceptible from the snow of the Mountain. Micah stopped.

From the snow bloomed a flower, pale, curled, desperate. A stem of wool held it in delicate balance above the cold earth from which it was rooted. Though a slight breeze touched it, the stem did not flutter, and the flower remained still. It was dead, encapsulated in a prison of ice, and its root dead with it. Zachary's lifeless face watched Micah from within the gentle hands of the White Mountain.

There was no time in this moment. The wind ceased to blow, and no sound could be heard as Micah fell to his knees. Only the snow continued to fall. Micah felt a terrible cry rise from his lungs and escape his mouth; it was lost into the clouds.

"My friend," he whispered as the awful cry abandoned his body. His words were sharp, and stung his ears, but amidst his tears he found the words would not be stopped. "My friend.

What have you done, to be so cruelly left here on this Holy Mountain? My friend, why have they done this to you, you who were so righteous in your cause? This Mountain, can it have judged so unfairly? The gods, could they be capable of such injustice?

"This hideous thing which has been done to you- it could not be done by a righteous hand! Did you not heed their warning, Zachary, and did you not sacrifice the summit for their jealousy?" Micah's words began to tumble, and spit froze in the corners of his mouth. "What have you done to him, for he was humble and not deserving of such an abominable end! He was good!" The tears clung to the corners of Micah's eyes. "He was good; by the gods he was good! He was good, as I could never be."

Micah withdrew his shaking hands and clutched at his chest. "Cruel gods, would you spare me this pain and let me fail here beside one greater than I? Would you return him his soul for one as wicked as mine? Would that not be justice; would that not be merciful? I surrender my desires, I surrender my soul, for his death is not worth any joy I might have enjoyed in this lifetime!"

The Mountain did not answer. Micah tore his eyes from his friend, and threw his head back to bear witness to the void. "I pray, all you who sit above, answer me! Why have you done this to him, why have you done this to me? Is this the outcome that you desired, does this sacrifice please you? A wolf is not capable of such injustice, the roaming bear not so cruel! Damn you all, and a curse upon this forsaken Mountain!"

Micah bore his teeth, and awaited destruction. But still the White Mountain was silent. The soft snow collected upon his pale face. Micah's flash of anger drained him; he felt his muscles loosen, and his neck go limp. His head fell forward, and Zachary's cloudy eyes once again met his. Micah was seized with a sudden bitter cold.

"My friend," Micah muttered in private audience. "Why did you follow me? Could you not see that I was so undeserving? I knew nothing but my own desires, and nothing of your own. I left you. I killed you. I knew it the moment you

123

turned away and I did not follow. But a wretch as I am, I could not ignore my soul. What I have done, it is unforgivable. I will not ask your apology; I would not accept it if it was given, for I am unworthy." Micah cradled his heads in his hands, and at last his reserves utterly failed him. He wept in the snow and his body convulsed with each sob.

"I am so lost, Zachary; there is nothing for me here, not in this land, or in the next. I thought perhaps together we would not be alone, but I see there is no company for men such as me. Your death, it is my future too. It was my black gift to you, to share in my penance. But we shall never find that which we seek, for what we seek cannot be found. A never-ending summit, that is what has laid claim to our souls. You died climbing it, as will I. I see it now, so clearly, as never before.

"If it is to be my fate, then so be it. It is better to die than to live under the influence of this treacherous soul. Why I have received it, perhaps in the next life I will know. But here, it has made me a dark and terrible thing, a creature of desire, a monster unfulfilled. And if the gods will not take justice into their hands, then I will.

"We will die together; my friend- you shall not be alone."

Micah collapsed into the snow.

SALVATION

The Mountain whispers along the wind, and by it its children listen. On that day I heard a tale of a seeker of the Mountain, of one who had failed upon its slopes, of one who was lost even as he had pursued its righteous summit. The wind rose and fell as the story was spun, rippling like a sheet of ice under the alpine sun. Even as my feet broke the crust of the Holy Mountain, the wind continued to speak.

"Come to the man of the Mountain," it said to me. "Come to the man who has left all, only to be left by all. For he is weary, and is not long for this world."

So I followed this call as it led me to the seeker. I could feel the anxiety in the air around me; the Mountain was growing desperate for its follower. And as I found the seeker, already the Mountain had begun to accept him into its skin. I pulled him from the snow, thanking the Mountain for its mercy, as the man breathed still. As I turned from the spot with him fastened to my sled, I saw that the seeker had not been alone. Another lay deep in the snow. But the Mountain had already laid claim to his soul.

My fellow seekers, this man is the one the Mountain spoke of. He is lost, he does not know the way. The gods have allowed him to suffer for his passion. The Mountain has denied him blessing, as it has many of us in our own time. He lies here in our home. His body is broken, his passion as well. In his sleep he cries for his companion, in his sleep he weeps for he feels betrayed.

Such pain, have we all not felt it? Those of us carried by none other than desire, how easily we are led astray. And those of us who are guided but without heart, how they have envied their energetic brothers and sisters. It is as written by those before, but remains wisdom to be rediscovered for an eternity.

Should we wish to alleviate pain from our brother? Do we wish to ease his burden? His form is miserable indeed. See how the black begins to migrate from the toes? Our seeker will have lost more than his companion by the end of the

125

night. Indeed, he has lost even the summit, which perhaps he coveted above all else. The Mountain told me of his terrible love, of his magnificent hate. He knows not why he must suffer. He knows not why he has been gifted with an uncompromising soul.

The soul, the spirit of a man, it is a gift indeed. How we have all doubted it, how I have doubt still! And can one be blamed for such anger, when the seeker is left so utterly alone? In company we have grown stronger, but think back, think back to the time when you were alone. It was not so easy then. We raged for answers, we burned for such truths. We were so disillusioned with the nature of the gods.

This man, this young seeker, this lover betrayed, he now needs our guidance. He is one of us, brothers and sisters. If he should come to see the light of purpose, if he should forgo his reckless ways, I would gladly join him on the Mountain. But it is not my day to climb, and so one of you must claim his burden. You shall plead his case before the Mountain and the gods. But it is his choice, and by his power alone that he shall climb. You must not forget it, and neither shall he.

ATONEMENT

This is the fate of the lover should he not reconcile the two elements of love: passion and purpose. For when separated, the passionate heart is fed by the fire but remains eternally lost, while the purposeful mind is destined to fail for lack of will. Only in this union can the seeker find lasting love: love of soul, love of self, love of life. Only in this union can he persevere great trial, and discover the purest joy. Like moths to the flame, the seekers flocked to deceitful images of love, and upon each other's charred bodies they will clamber to truer sources. Upon each other's bodies, they must learn, or they too will perish.

The beating heart of the White Mountain faded gently into the abyss. Warmth slipped with it, replaced by a dead cold. Voices reverberated in his dreams, sometimes drawing quite close, sometimes drifting away. The darkness fled, and a red light danced in the void. Then it left, and for some great time the world was darkness. But the darkness was cruel. He felt flashes of terrible pain, and cried out in agony; however, there was nothing to hear his voice. He shared the black with no one. He floundered in the ebony sea for an infinity.

Then infinity subsided. The flickering red returned, and Micah fixated on it. The darkness broke, and the flicker became a brilliant flash. The light was unbearable, but he could not escape it. After a few painful moments, it withdrew, and before him a new image formed.

He lay in a bed heavily layered with wools, placed in a humble cell constructed of crude stone. The room was dark, for it had no windows, and through its chiseled walls the low moan of the wind could be heard. A tattered gray curtain marked the only entrance to the chamber, opposite to the bed. Beside the curtain, a small fire burned. Micah struggled to focus his eyes. A hand gripped the torch, and its flame hinted at the face that held it. A blue face with flint eyes hovered from within an aura of its shadow.

"Welcome to Eulhstan, the stone-temple. You have been asleep for several nights, stricken with the Mountain's fever."

The visitor's voice was smooth, young, and distinctly feminine. Micah immediately recognized it as a voice that had occupied many of his late feverish dreams. Micah opened his mouth to speak, but found his voice dry, and his throat sore. The visitor immediately swooped forward, and with a gentle hand brought a water skin to his cracked lips.

"You are weak, do not speak." Her voice was commanding, and so Micah obliged. As he fought down several mouthfuls of warm water he studied his visitor, but she gave him little more than a cautious smile in return. "My brother carried you down from the slopes of the Mountain. You have been treated for your wounds, and will survive your climb. You should thank the Mountain for speaking on your behalf."

Micah's head still swam, and her words failed to cling to his consciousness. A burble of emotions caught him, but his mind remained dry. The woman sat at the edge of his bed. Her eyes slipped through him, past the cold stone and into the flurry of snow that murmured beyond the walls. Her guarded smile fell, but she did not appear to be angry. With an almost inaudible sigh, she stood, collected the water skin, and stepped through the curtain.

When Micah woke again, his bed was visited by another, this time a man dressed in dark robes and bearing familiar painted skin. The man turned his blue face to Micah as he noticed him awaken.

"It is good to finally meet, dear seeker," the blue face bowed. "My name is Osric. You have met my sister, Godwina. She has tended to you without end; I hope that it has eased your suffering."

Osric bowed his head again, but this time directed Micah's attention towards his feet with an open hand. Micah followed his hand with his eyes slowly, still caught in a state of mild delirium. A pale foot protruded from the bedsheets, a foot he noticed that supported only three fluttering toes. It was curious to Micah, and as he looked he found that he could choose to wriggle each toe. The fog began to clear, and soon

128

the weight of his condition impacted him like a hammer. Micah felt the bile rise in his throat, he leapt forward in his bed but found that his body was pathetically weak and merely collapsed back into his sheets from the effort.

"What, what has been done to me?" Micah battled each word past his shattered lips with a stale tongue.

Osric lifted his head from the bow, which Micah realized was not meant of respect but of pity. Osric's eyes betrayed his great empathy, though indeed he made no effort to conceal it. They watered as he spoke.

"You have lost much to the Mountain. But what loss of the body can compare to that of the soul? Seeker, the Mountain shared with me your story. Yours is a story we of the stone-temple know well, for here we are brothers and sisters of the Mountain. It is why you are here, as you were spared by the Mountain."

With every second that passed Micah emerged further from his fever, and every second brought a more horrible memory. Osric's words gave him his final push from the safety of his blindfold, and back into the naked light. And at Osric's last words, Micah was purged by a gargling wail. His body convulsed as it remembered the cold snow, his eyes shut tight as the white face of his companion haunted his vision.

Osric waited quietly beside his bedside until his fits subsided. Micah soon lost his energy and his shouts deteriorated into weak sobbing. His hands and feet tingled, and his stomach turned endlessly, holding him at the perpetual brink of vomiting. Only until Micah had sufficiently quieted did Osric venture again to speak.

"Why do we climb the Mountain, fellow seeker? Is such pain our only reward? Can suffering, can death, be worth the answer?" His face became stern, rigid as the great stone bulwarks of The Divide. "Do you wish to finally have your questions answered? Do you wish to satisfy the longing of your soul?"

Despite his tears, Micah racked with a scornful laugh. Osric remained stoic, his question laid bare. When Micah realized his sincerity, his caustic anger boiled. "Do you see what has become of me?" he screamed. "Do you see what an

129

atrocity I have committed? Did the White Mountain tell you that I left him to die, because I desired such answers? No, I do not desire these answers! No more will I sacrifice so much only to bleed and to draw blood; I tell you that there will be no more suffering at the cause of these hands! And how heartless you were to pull me from my rightful tomb, how pitilessly do you serve the Mountain's bidding! If you truly knew my story, you would have left me to perish, as must be the god's intent."

"Have you already forgotten your passion, tired seeker? Search yourself, will you ever abandon the Mountain? I ask again, do you wish to satisfy the longing of your soul? Do you wish to climb the White Mountain?"

"Heartless," Micah spluttered. "Insatiable, heartless monster! I have ignored too many warnings, I have proceeded a man without senses, and you would encourage my blundering? I should have been satisfied with my gifts, I should have been humble, and I should have bowed to the gods!"

"To do so would be to ignore your greatest gift. Would you deny the gods their creation? Would you crawl back into your valley, and squander that which is available to you? You have this chance, seeker, to finally meet your passion. You seek the blessing of the White Mountain. Its summit will deliver nothing less, I tell you, for I have stood upon it."

Osric's voice dropped low, rumbling like the tumble of snow over the mountainside. "I have stood on the summit of the White Mountain, our most holy summit, and it is there that I received the blessing of sight. Where before I was lost, there I knew purpose. Where before I knew only pain, there I knew joy. It is there brother, that we all find our love. It is there, that this long journey must end."

There was nothing that Micah could say. Through his mask of hate, he wilted, for he could fight no more. Nothing he could do, but to plead. "Osric, your words are for another greater than I. Your words are for those who are deserving. Perhaps the gods did give me a gift, but I am not strong enough to receive it. And so in my weakness, I killed one who was deserving. The Mountain spoke of Zachary, surely it told you of his story. What you found on the Mountain, it is not what you sought. I am not what the Mountain desired to save."

"No seeker, I do not know for what purpose the gods took the life of your friend, but it is you whom I sought. Do not hide from them now. I ask again, and for the last time, do you wish to climb the White Mountain?"

Micah tried to put up his final defense, but it was easily crushed, and with a shuddering gasp he surrendered. "Yes," he whispered at along last. He thought for a long moment, the last of his anger ebbing away. "A creature as I am for admitting it, I still wish to climb the Mountain."

"And why should you summit the Mountain?" Osric's eyes bored into him.

The question felt as a sharp blow to one unguarded, and Micah nearly lashed out once more. He swallowed back his anger before answering, "I do not deserve it. I should not summit the White Mountain."

Osric leaned back, however his eyes continued to dig into Micah's. "Then you shall not summit."

"What am I to say, that I deserve to summit? That I am worthy of blessing?" Micah could not restrain himself any longer.

"What makes it a question of what one deserves? Seeker, you deserve nothing. Make your case for the gods, why should you receive the blessing of sight?"

"I should receive such a blessing, because I have suffered at their hands, and I should know why I must suffer! I should know why I have been burdened with so impatient a soul, a soul that is forever insatiable, a soul that brings me to destruction, of myself, and of others. And if I do climb the Mountain, then I should know if it is mere foolishness to tempt the mighty summit, or if it does somehow pay tribute to the gods and to my soul. For my weary soul, so you have tempted me to believe it throughout all this pain."

Osric's eyes softened. "I will not accompany you up the Mountain. My sister, Godwina, she will do this for you. But you are still weak, and are in great need of rest. I hope that in short time, dear seeker, I will help you to find your answers."

In the days that followed Micah was nursed back to his feet. Only Osric and Godwina spoke to him, the latter in few words. But the remainder of the temple remained silent as they watched him battle for balance upon his wounded feet. He found meals prepared in the mornings and the evenings, and was left to his own devices for much of the day. In that time, he would wander the low slopes of the White Mountain. He watched its summit without end, until the last day of the season had come. Osric spoke, their packs were filled, and together Micah and Godwina walked out into the snow.

REUNION

The seeker departs once more, though his head hangs with the memory of the past. He carries his suffering up the Mountain, and hopes to discover his joy. His passion still burns brightly, but there too is wisdom to be found in pain. He shall not forget the bodies of his brothers. And so he climbs for blessing; he climbs for sight. He does not yet embrace any love; now timidly does he return to his betrothed.

The White Mountain allowed a light snow to fall the morning of their departure. It fell long into the day, keeping the air cool and the snow firm to their step. They climbed in silence, but it was not any social obstruction that kept them from conversation. Micah had grown accustomed to Godwina's long periods of quiet, and on this day preferred to remain in his thoughts. His body soon remembered the dull ache of ascent, of the sweat that trapped to his chest, and the sting of the cold mountain air.

They ascended the Mountain via the west ridge, for the stone-temple was perched just north of the rocky wall that guarded it from the south. The route was well known to the men of the temple, as Osric had informed Micah. However, it was wrought with its own challenges; though the west slopes managed to overcome the mighty rampart to the south, above this it cut sharply into the sky. The glittering wall of ice could be skirted to the north or to the south, the latter as Micah had passed so many days before.

"The route via the south glacier is a route for the dead," Osric had stated with finality. "Though the ice is mostly passable, it encounters a separation that cuts deeper than the eye can penetrate. There is no crossing here, though many have tried. Many more still have descended here in desperation only to be swallowed by such a maw."

The only alternative to the south was therefore the north, and this required a long traverse to the north face of the

White Mountain. The summit of the Mountain was a citadel, surrounded by high walls save for a solitary gate. This gateway, revered by the monks as the Pilgrim's Ladder, slipped between the walls of the north face. It was to be their passage.

"We shall sleep tonight on the west ridge," Godwina broke the silence finally. They had been walking for many hours, unperturbed by weather or difficult conditions. "The Mountain smiles upon our first day."

Upon the mighty shoulder of the White Mountain, above the black walls that guarded it from below, they cut a small cave into the snow. Godwina spread a thick waxed tarpaulin inside, and as the night fell they wrapped themselves tightly in wool. The snow continued to fall gently outside, even as the sun dropped below the horizon. Godwina's breath shortly assumed a slow rhythm, but Micah could not find sleep so easily.

"Though you have believed it for so very long, you were not destined to be only a seeker. Indeed, it will always be part of you, however it is but one gift of your soul." Osric had stood beside him days before their departure. They were outside the stone-temple, sharing in the sight of the White Mountain. "To seek, it is how we find love. By seeking, we can let loose our desperate passions. Those who cannot seek so, how can they ever hope to find true love? That is why the passionate are blessed, though they suffer greatly. It is not for all to recognize it."

"Why then do I receive such passion, why not others? If it is truly a gift as you say, why then was I made for it?"

"How can I know your heart, or the hearts of others? Do I commune with the gods? How then can I know this great journey, as set by the gods above? If you were to ask them, and hear the answer, would you be satisfied? You judge the world and the heavens above, but you are not immortal. We who are so blind cannot judge."

Micah closed his eyes, and awoke to the movements of Godwina beside him. They emerged from their shelter, and ate a large breakfast in the dawn light. The Hall flashed orange below them, with its snow cradling the fire of the sun. There was no cloud on the horizon, and The Divide held its breath. Godwina nodded approvingly towards the summit.

They gathered their belongings, and resumed their climb of the White Mountain.

"Indeed, even what is holy, and what is shameful, they are not always so distinct in our mortal eyes. What then can a man do, if he cannot understand his gods, and he cannot trust himself? Is there no compass to guide the seeker, is there no summit to be had? Such a man is lost; he wanders endlessly. His soul is starving, and he cannot feed it. Like a wolf he consumes all the gifts and blessings of this world, so carefully given by the gods. But they are nothing to him, tasteless, and worse: poisonous. He cannot see. He cannot feel. He neither lives in this world or the next."

"I have seen him, and it terrifies me to remember."

On the second day of their climb the wind began to hum with the rise of the sun. The light burned the snow, and threatened them with its glare. Godwina removed a pair of leather straps, each cut with two narrow slits, and helped Micah to fasten one before his eyes. They shielded their bodies with cloth, though it caused them to pant from the heat. What skin that remained exposed, they greased with a heavy blue paint.

They pushed for the ice wall above the west shoulder, and followed gentle slopes on sticky snow. Though Micah was forced to pause often to catch his breath and give rest to his legs, the climb moved quickly, and he had begun to recognize a small spark in his chest. With each step it triggered, with every breath it too breathed. But it did not catch fire.

"It is good to remember such a man. He does not see that the gods have provided us with a bearing, one that not only guides but rewards. It is the greatest gift of the gods, dear seeker. There is a reason why we all climb the White Mountain, a reason why our souls cry for nourishment. There is food for them yet. But how can I explain it to one who has perceived only pain?

"Tell me, dear seeker, why is it that you entered The Divide? What was it that you sought, if not for the great summits?"

"The City of the Gods," Micah murmured into the winds. "I doubted, and it consumed me. I desired to see it, with my own eyes."

Osric laughed. "It is a common goal, more common than you might think. Tell me seeker, if I were to tell you that the City cannot be found, not by man, would you abandon your quest?"

"I think I abandoned that quest long ago."

The hot sun softened the snow under their feet, and their legs sunk to the hips. Each step became strenuous, even on the low-angled terrain. Godwina did not once complain, nor did she sing the Mountain's praises. Her face was set hard, and she did not break stride. Micah fought to swim up the ruin of snow in her wake.

"A young man's quest is to find the City. Some claim that they have, some may even believe it. To walk among the gods, to commune in their dining halls, an honor indeed for the noblest of us! To find the City is to be a god, to leave this life and promote into the next.

"Hear my words, for I tell you that some summits cannot be reached! Does that mean they should not be climbed? Therefore, I say, that it is foolish to intend to find the City, but righteous indeed to seek it! Your gift, dear seeker, your passion, you can grow closer to the City than any without it! Is that not a gift indeed, is that not nourishment for your soul?"

The pulpit of ice soared into the cloudless sky above them. Micah strained his neck and tottered in his footsteps to sight its termination, but he could see very little through the leather wrapped over his eyes. He saw the ice sparkle and flash as the sun straddled between it and the sky; he saw the rays bursting their abominable heat over the frozen landscape. He marveled at the sharp cold of his feet, and at the steaming sweat that ran from his brow. A slight breeze caused him to shiver and draw his coverings close, but as it abated he soon found himself wishing for another to grace his skin. He looked to Godwina, and saw with some surprise that she had withdrawn her blindfold.

"It is not safe-" he started, before remembering that Godwina needed no reminder of the danger. She did not face

136

the wall of ice, but instead her gaze traced the rib of the west ridge, to the stone-temple nestled deep in its seat of snow, and wandered the slopes down to rest in the bosom of the Hall. Micah pulled back the leather and squinted into the consequent glare. "What is it that you see?"

Godwina did not answer immediately, and Micah waited patiently as he had grown accustomed to. When she spoke, it was but a breath of air, light, transitory, and from an origin unknown. "A gift." She flashed her eyes to Micah's. "Here I receive it. Why cannot you?"

"What manner of gift is this?" Micah was indignant.

Osric's voice rose to a veritable shout. He leapt to his feet, cast his arms open wide and with clenched fingers seemed to embrace the image of the White Mountain before him. "Dearest seeker, this gift is the blood that runs in our veins, the very fire that burnt in our hearts, it is the rhythm of our wandering souls! You have felt it, the Mountain told me! I have felt it, as I do now before the holy offspring of the gods!" The wind swelled like the tide, and Osric laughed as it splashed over his feet. He swayed over a precipice, his toes wriggling over blue darkness. The White Mountain opened under him, but he had eyes only for its summit. The stone-temple was perched very far from them now.

"Seeker, what is it that the true lover remembers in his bride? What is it that you have seen, even on the slopes of the Twisted Peak, that which is the same here on the White Mountain? Oh, perhaps it is too early for you, too early to see it. But I tell you, as I have heard your story, I have seen it for you, even if you cannot. It is the City, Micah! It is the greatest gift of the gods; it is why they have given you such a passionate soul! It is not good, nor is it evil, for it is both of these things, good and evil, pain and joy, Twisted and White!"

The wind stopped, and Osric teetered above the abyss. He looked down, into the cavernous pit, into the blue mouth that was lipped with icy teeth and a tongue of fluted snow. The air around him seemed to buckle and freeze before slipping into the maw for one sucking breath. But then he looked up, over the crystalline fields of white, over the towers of ice and the fortresses of stone. He looked up until his eyes fell upon the mighty crown of the King which burned in the sun like a beacon for The Divide, like a golden chalice offered by earth to the gods.

And Osric whispered. "Beauty. For the faces of heaven burn too brightly; they gave us beauty, that we might see them still."

Godwina shook her head, but did not respond further. She merely chewed her lip as she drew back the leather strap across her eyes and tied it within a tangle of dark hair. "Come, we must make camp on the north face. Tomorrow the Mountain will judge us." Godwina spoke to the winds, and Micah strained to hear it. He drew the cords of his pack tight, and slumped back into her footsteps.

They walked until the sun fell under the western rib of the Hall, and only the high walls of the White Mountain still glowed orange in the dying light. Soon even the reflection of ice failed to illuminate the snow, and the Mountain was swallowed in a sheet of darkness. They stopped to dig a crude shelter under a slight outcropping of stone, and huddled within. The wind had begun to hum through The Divide, and with it rode the withering cold of the late season.

Micah waited for sleep to overtake him that evening, but found that it would not come. He rubbed his stiff feet, fumbling with the cavernous empty spaces between his toes, uncomfortably few in number.

As he lay thinking a soft voice murmured out from beside him. "What is it that he has said you will find on the summit?" Godwina rolled over in her blanket, knocking a dusting of ice from the ceiling.

Though Micah could not see her, he still peered into her imagined face. "Beauty," he whispered.

The winds outside had grown to a whistle. "Why does he say this; why does he push himself to such places? Why does he push others to the same ends?" There was a note of concern in Godwina's voice that surprised Micah.

"The gift is only for those who summit, is it not?"

"Such are the words of my brother," she replied testily. Micah heard her breath quicken in the darkness. "He is not wrong Micah. If you summit, you will receive a gift. But the gift of sight is not always as we anticipate it."

Micah lay on the tarpaulin, his eyes gliding along the slopes that waited above their ceiling of snow. "I have nothing now Godwina, nothing but the Mountain. If I lose this too, what reason do I have to continue?"

"You had a home Micah, and you chose this. Do not forget that."

Her words bit the air, stinging Micah far more than any bitter gale. He felt his face grow hot, and was resigned to silence. Godwina allowed the whistle of the Mountain to occupy their little shelter, to which Micah listened as he waited for sleep to find him. He waited for a voice, for a whisper, but none would come, and sleep would not claim either of them that evening.

Osric turned to Micah. "Because neither the heart nor the mind could provide guidance to man, Micah, we were gifted our souls. What do our souls seek? They seek to experience the divine beauty. This beauty, this experience that drips with passion and purpose, all of mankind is awed by it, all of mankind remembers it, and all of mankind hungers for it. Our pilgrimage to this holy summit is to be our suffering, but at its peak we are blessed! Only here may we see the divine beauty that encompasses both the pain and the joy!"

Osric's hair whipped around his head in a frenzy, and his coat flapped under the gale that steamed from the blue mouth of the White Mountain. He wore a triumphant smile, his teeth a white bastion amidst his skin painted blue.

But Micah did not smile. "Tell me, Osric, is then the suffering of my brother meant for my pilgrimage? Did he die that I and others might find such beauty?" The grin faltered on Osric's lips, but he did not interject as Micah carefully found his words. "I will climb the White Mountain. I have nothing; I must see as you have seen. But if this is the divine will, then I say it is not beautiful. And I will reject the gods forever, and this Holy Mountain."

Micah walked alone through the snow.

ASCENSION

Now the seeker begins to see the object of true love, for it is that which deserves his passion, and that which dictates his purpose. And so he moves towards its light, and the love in his heart begins to glow. It has taken him through the dark forest, scorched his hand with hellfire, and now drags him to the top of the coldest mountain. And the lover is thankful. For now, he sees; he sees that beauty of his lover is lost without his pain and his sacrifice. He sees that to fear the mountain and climb: that is to truly love the mountain.

There was no light when Godwina gently shook Micah awake. He could hear nothing but the soft bellow of his breath into the cold. The ice crackled around him as his rolling body crushed the delicate crystals that had formed as he slept, clutching his huddled body in the white hand of the Mountain. Godwina slipped out of the shelter, dragging her leather pack out with her.

Micah peered out into the muted blackness. The darkness waited above a faint platform of snow that glowed under the night sky. But suddenly the heavens were no longer black, for they gathered a sparkling choir of stars. One by one they assembled above, each providing a guiding light into the blanket of snow below. And they whispered together as he drew himself out onto the slopes of the White Mountain.

The summit pinnacle towered above them, a mottled shade of black that held no light save for a single ribbon of snow that cleaved the darkness in two. It was a bridge of starlight between two islands in a turbulent sea.

"A ladder from man to the gods," Godwina whispered.

Micah took a step forward. The pinnacle swelled before him, enveloping the entirety of his vision, demanding the passion of his agonized soul. It was before him as never before, the crown of the White Mountain, that which promised him hope, and that which had destroyed so much. His heart flashed with fear and cold, but his soul rose to sputter into the life the old flame that there still lingered. And before the White Mountain, Micah spoke.

"I am here for your blessing. I am here for your sight. Bless me, and I will listen. Grant me your beauty, and I will continue to seek it. I want to see the faces that made me. I want to nourish the soul that drives me. If this is who I am to be, then tell me here, or my soul will be forever lost."

Micah's legs slipped into motion. The snow felt like feathers beneath his feet. The sharp air broke against the fire that burned throughout his body. He felt his breath tighten, and his heart pound in his chest. The ladder rose before him, and in one motion Micah drew two iron hooks and swung them into its spine. The metal bit into the ice, and held. Micah took an uneasy step up, kicking repeatedly into the ice to find adequate purchase. He withdrew each hook in turn, plunging them ever higher into the bridge, ascending as he had been instructed by Osric at the stone-temple.

The Mountain was quiet as it watched the pilgrim climb, and the assembly of the Hall acquiesced to its silence. The Knights watched in jealousy as he rose higher than even their mightiest pinnacles. They stood in rows, shuffling in behind one another, wrinkling their stony faces to see the ladder illuminated in the night. He rose as a point of darkness in the river of starlight, steady in his approach, not faulting in his step, not surrendering to the fears that he held. Though he soared between the White Mountain's furrowed brows, he did not look down. He climbed, and as he climbed the stars above him flashed and rippled in the sky. They were singing, and his soul sang with them. Micah climbed to the summit of the White Mountain.

BEAUTY

Is the face of his lover worth such suffering? The lover cannot know until he has seen. And to see, this requires incredible pain. For he who sacrifices the most for his lover lifts her veil the highest. It is his opportunity to suffer for her. And it is his reward that he should love her with the entirety of his immortal soul.

The Hall looked closely as the pilgrim made his way to the gleaming cap of their King. He seemed not to move, and yet before the night began its retreat he had placed himself on the mighty summit. There he stood, an iris encircled by starlight, as much a star to those below as the stars that hung an infinity away. And the Hall held its breath, and looked to the heavens above.

Micah's body made a soft impression on the cold head of the White Mountain. He sat on the frozen snow, for there were no rocks to be found. His body still burned from the climb, and he melted into the ice. He worked to regain control of his breathing, for his chest heaved from the climb, and then lifted his eyes from the snow. Micah looked to the south, he looked to the Hall, and he looked to see The Divide laid bare before him.

The Knights of The Divide rose in their columns, but they no longer pointed jealous faces. They bent their heads, and atop each helm the light of heaven was caught in snow. Their armor sparkled a celestial white as it coated their shields, outlined their swords, and ran in ribbons through their stony flesh. That night before the heavens The Divide was laced in cold starlight. It marched from east to west, north to south, and as the Knights rose further from their King their glowing armor became fine points on the horizon, and at this intersection heaven and earth bled into one another, merged by the darkness that ran between the light they shared.

Micah no longer recognized The Divide. Nor did he recognize his perch. As he stared, the frontiers of The Divide curled skywards towards the heavens. He found himself sitting on the inside of a hollow globe, one that gently blurred upwards from his own patch of starlight and into the tiny patches that hung above. The light of the White Mountain was no longer received but exchanged with the heaven. For it too was a point of heaven to the stars above, to the mighty range that wrapped the inside of this holy dominion. Micah rose to his feet. His legs trembled beneath him, and as he rolled his head back he stumbled in the snow.

"Have you always been so close, though you felt so far?" Micah's words escaped his lips in small clouds, only to fade into the night sky. "Were you here when I climbed the Twisted Peak? Were you here when Zachary fell? Did he see your faces?"

The stars below and above flashed and flickered. Micah shook, and his eyes welled with tears. "My soul, you have brought me to this moment. You pushed me from my home, away from the valley, over The Divide, and atop this most holy summit. Be free of my mortal body, leave me here, and be at peace! This is your home, for your power will surely destroy me." Micah choked, and the tears began to tumble down his cheeks. They were warm but left streaks of cold.

"I thank you for what you have given me, for I would never have seen so much beauty without your guiding light. I am just a man, and yet you show me heaven! I was weak from fear, and yet you gave me courage! You were my greatest blessing, though I was blind to see it!"

Micah looked to the starlight beneath him. He looked to the starlight around him, and to the starlight above him. His voice cracked as it rose to a shout. "Take it from me now, you have given me your blessing! Oh fearsome, merciful gods, so much beauty might blind a simple man as I! I have followed you, and you have given me sight. I am blessed!"

The stars glowed like coals, and the White Mountain was radiant among them. The darkness around them was absolute, deeper than the deepest pit of the Mountain. It swam in currents around the light, blood passed between heaven and earth. It swirled and splashed around Micah's island. As he watched, it clutched his heart with terror, and in desperation he locked his eyes with a single star that hung directly above.

"Take it from me now, so that I might not tempt your wrath! Take it from me now, so that I would not spoil your sanctuary with my presence! Take it from me now, for with it I do not know where to go!" Micah's legs quivered and then collapsed beneath him. He sank his knees into the snow, and his open hands fell into his lap. But he did not lose sight of the star above.

"I am but a man. I do not deserve to see your face. If you take this from me, I will live simply. I will live as a man should, not in the realm of gods, but in the lands far below. But if you leave this soul within me, I will not forget what I have seen. How can I forget such terror? How can I forget such joy? How can I forget such beauty? It will drive me to heaven, it will drive me always to see. I long to see your face, I long to see your beauty. It is worth the pain, to glimpse as I do now. It is the pain, to see as I do now. My soul, my love, it is yours! Take it, and leave the man behind! It is my gift to you, freely given at last!"

The stars rippled and shook through his tears, and they were joined by brilliant arms of light. But as Micah's voice echoed into the Hall, the heavens did not answer. Not even the wind touched the crown of the White Mountain that evening. Micah sat shivering in the cold, but he would not leave his post. Though his body begged him to return to warmth, he would not grant it. For he felt the fires of his soul still boiling in his chest. It extended its roots deeply into his body, through his fingers and toes, burning the same familiar flame.

And so he waited until the night at last began to break into dawn. Though the great body of the sun did not yet peek over the mountains of The Divide, its soft light gently unrolled the heavens and earth. No longer were they engaged in an embrace, for the horizon cut a jagged edge between blacks and blues, and the stars began to recede into the sky. Soon they were lost, not to be found until the sun again abandoned its vigil. And all the while Micah watched that now empty place where the star once burned.

"Did you see?"

The voice teased Micah from his fixation. He blinked, and turned to see Godwina sitting on the summit behind him. Her face and body glowed by morning fire.

"Yes." Micah thought for a moment. "I begged them Godwina. I begged them to take it from me. My soul. But here it lies." He placed a hand on his chest.

Godwina graced him with a slight smile. "Yes, there it lies still."

"I am a man. How can a man see the gods? How can a mortal live beside the immortal?" He turned back to face the sunrise, to let its rays bring warmth to his cold face. "I thought it a mistake. But they would not take it from me."

"It is a gift Micah. Do not turn it away."

The sky was alight with the light of the sun. It drew its orange body over the horizon, and its light broke over the tallest heads of The Divide, though its valleys remained in darkness. Clouds cowered within these valleys, burning as the light pressed down ever more. But the sky held no clouds, and was as blue as the deep ice of the mountains. Micah and Godwina held a reverent silence as the sun gathered itself in the sky.

"Come, the Ladder will be softening soon. It is time to descend."

Godwina gathered her tools and lowered herself off the summit. Micah gave one last look into the sky above, then gathered his own tools, and stepped from the summit of the White Mountain.

145

MOVEMENT

Where now will the new lover go? Will he stay and follow this image of his bridge? Will he forget her face, and lose his way? His journey is never complete, her face never fully known. The City remains to be seen, and his soul will always hunger for more. But might he be comfortable with that hunger, with that insatiable appetite? No longer is he a seeker, for he knows now what he seeks. He is a lover, imbued with violent passion and rigid purpose. But how the lover offers his love, and how the bride reveals herself to his gestures, that is not for men such as myself to decide.

The Divide was full of whispers when Micah and Godwina stepped off of the Pilgrim's Ladder. A gentle wind slipped between its many fingers and many thorns, sharing knowledge of the dawn's ascent. The White Mountain did not partake in these whispers, and with holy silence allowed its travelers to descend under a clear blue sky. There were no hindrances to their departure from the summit, and even the snow was soft and gracious beneath their feet.

Before the sun could stand high in the sky, Micah and Godwina found themselves perched on a rocky outcropping that hung over the southern slopes. From their vantage, the stone-temple could be seen nestled just beyond the rolling western slopes. They shared a small meal as Godwina scrutinized their descent path. But when she spoke, Micah realized that her mind was elsewhere. There was an edge to her voice, a sharpness that he could not identify.

"Is something wrong, Godwina?" Her shoulders stiffened, and she turned from the slopes to meet his eyes.

"What will you do now that you have seen? Will you remain here, with us, to continue this pilgrimage? To follow my brother?" Her eyes were earnest, but her face betrayed no emotion.

"I had not considered it until now," Micah said slowly. "But your brother is wise, and I am a man without a home."

Godwina's eyes flashed. "I chose to leave, and I will not risk hurting my family again," Micah said, noticing her glare. "This beauty is wonderful, and terrifying to me. It has captivated my soul! Should I not pursue it?" He smiled, but Godwina's face had become blank once more.

"So you will stay," she said flatly.

"If I am welcome to, I believe that I must."

Godwina's shoulders sagged, and she brought a hand to her forehead. To Micah's surprise, he saw her features twist with anxiety, and lines etch with frustration. But before he could speak, she interrupted with a strangled voice.

"You would be like my brother, then? To stay here forever, always to seek the gift of the White Mountain? The gift of all mountains Micah, the hard face of beauty?" Tears welled in the corners of her eyes, but they did not fall.

Micah was aghast, and his words trembled as he spoke. "Is it not the face of beauty? Do you not see it for yourself?"

"Of course I have seen it!" Godwina's voice fell, and her tone softened. "But Micah, it is not the face of beauty, as my brother would say. It is but one of the faces of beauty, one of the faces of the gods, one of many! Would you stay here, to worship that one face, when there are more to behold?"

"Godwina, if this is true, then why does my soul call me here? Why did it lead me to such beauty, if it was not meant to be my pursuit?"

Godwina did not answer immediately, but shook her head and turned from Micah towards the stone-temple. She clasped her hands tightly in her lap. "It is true Micah; I know it because I have seen these faces. They live high in the mountains, and low in the deep valleys. They live in the trees, in the water, in pain and in joy. They live in me and in you. They live in the temple, in my love for my brother and his love for me. He does not see them, but for the White Mountain. Do not be like my brother, do not stay here to worship a mountain. There is more beauty to be found Micah, if only you would allow your soul to follow it."

A gentle murmur of wind snuck under the watchful eye of the White Mountain. It carried their words through the Hall, along blue rivers and ramparts of stone. It carried them through The Divide, and into the valleys, through fields of grass and wide open spaces that stretched out under the sun. It carried them to strange lands of which men had never seen, and down chimneys of homes where children and grandparents played. It tickled Micah's skin and danced around his nose. He took a breath, and the fire within him blazed into life.

"I am not finished with the mountains. I have not yet crossed The Divide." He looked to the west, to the walls of the stone-temple. "But I cannot cross if I am to stay here."

Godwina's countenance rounded, and a tentative grin crept into her lips. "Then go," she said. "Go, listen to your soul. Pursue the stony faces of beauty if you must, but do not do it here. Do not stop, Micah- do not ignore your soul."

"Thank you Godwina. Thank you for taking me here. Though I go today, perhaps one day I will return. I hope that this is not our last time together." Micah's face was bright, and his body felt tense with anticipation.

"Travel well, Micah. Go with the gods. There, you will find beauty."

They parted ways on the shoulders of the White Mountain. Godwina turned to the stone-temple, and Micah turned north, as he always had. The horizon marched with Knights, high and small, round and sharp, each bearing mighty arms of ice and snow. Micah saw them; he wondered at their summits, he felt their terror, his body ached from the labors of their passages, and he marveled at the beauty that traced every rampart of snow, every pinnacle of stone, and every dark precipice that they held. And he moved north, as his soul only knew how.

IV. the City of the Gods

TIME

It was cold even in the lowest valleys of The Divide. No longer did they blossom with wildflowers, no longer did they run with grass of deep green that splashed about scattered playgrounds of stone, but instead they were choked with billows of white snow. The sky was heavy with clouds, and each day they dripped their cold offering to the land below. The rivers froze, and only small currents skirted underneath sheets of thick ice. The valleys were quiet as they were gently entombed in whiteness, for in those days no creature sang. The valleys were occupied only by the wind, and there it seldom spoke above a whisper.

Micah remained in these valleys during this cold season, for he did not dare tempt the mighty summits that surrounded him. He traveled very little, and spent most of his time catching small game and warding away the encroaching frost. When the snow became too deep even for light travel, he built a meager cabin and resigned himself to its comforts. He enjoyed each evening with a bright fire, and was forced to maintain it for the duration of the night. On some days the cold still passed through his thickest furs, and Micah would not leave his cabin nor would he let his fire die, for without it he would succumb to the winter. On these days he ate very little, and had nothing to do but to ruminate beside the flames. The erratic dance of the fire drew his mind elsewhere, conjuring images of rocky points, of stars in the sky, and of wide valleys far below.

The onslaught of winter brought the fear and pain of the mountains to the valleys down below. They rode on the backs of galloping clouds and needling winds that howled across toothy passes and icy summits. Micah watched the mountains as each battled the heavens alone. They were choked by cloud, blasted with ice, swept by the wind. At night he was awoken by their rumblings as heaven ripped away at their flesh. Micah cried out in the night when he was afraid, he huddled beside the flame, he begged the gods to abate lest his own valley be crushed in the ruin of the mountainside. Each morning he would emerge to see a landscape transfigured; deep scars marked the faces of familiar peaks, tall trees vanished under the snow, mighty boulders that once stood proud atop the high shoulders lay broken in the valleys below.

The winter bared the rotting white teeth of The Divide, offspring of the earth yet glorified in their pursuit of heaven above. Though they faced a daily crucible of snow, they remained proud, not yielding to the powers that cast them down. In the dawn light they thrust their snow-blown faces into the sun, vying for radiance in the eternal darkness of winter. As the clouds swarmed their heads they hardened their white bodies and prayed again for morning to come, that the light would once again break the clouds and grace their lonely summits. And when the solitary peak thrust its head out of the dark and terrible clouds, when the light of the summit emanated from the mountain's blessed crown over the sorrowful land, Micah's breath abandoned him. His soul joined the mountain in those moments, celebrating its joy despite the long winter, and in the long winter.

For because the period of snow is long in The Divide, Micah soon lost count of the days. The whites did not change, they only grew and receded. But on one unassuming day, they ceased to grow. The waters of the river began to flow, and the patter of meltwater from the rocks and bushes permeated the air. The frozen growth spread its leaves and pushed its foliage through weak layers of snow. The last icicles dropped from the wood of Micah's home, and larger game took to the forests. Micah was no longer trapped by the land.

He began to push further from his simple home, making camp among the high lakes, leaving footsteps over tall passes, and even touching lower peaks that had already lost their helms of snow. The valleys became vibrant and green, the wildflowers exploded in the basins, and the birds again sang in the trees. His soul pushed him north once again, but at a slow pace. He explored as he moved, his curiosity tempting him into remote gorges, untouched forests, and lonely passes. And he saw no one, for he moved not over trail but over land. The Divide offered its virgin passages to him and he graciously accepted them.

The seasons turned as he walked, the frost came again and then went. He learned the faces of the mountains through them; he learned to recognize their winter beards of snow and their summer chins of stone. He learned their defenses and their weaknesses, and he cherished them for both. He waded through whites and greens, over ice and flowers, and bathed by the blaring sun and whip of the wind.

There was no record of time save for the wrinkles that multiplied in his skin. The Divide did not age, it circulated, rebirthed from snow, wiped clean by the rivers and by the rains. Each spring the mountains flashed clean, youthful faces, and each fall they slipped quietly back into their tombs. In the summer Micah watched as the creatures of The Divide celebrated its cradle, and each winter he watched as they disappeared. He did not count the seasons. And so they slipped under his nose, and he made no effort to stop them, for he was content to wander ever north in The Divide.

Where there was beauty, his soul was contented to roam. It pushed him through pain and through pleasure, bathing in the rhythm of time, blurring each into one. They became one, united by beauty that was in their soft juxtaposition, which worked its way into their feathered edges. He saw winter by the opaque of summer, and summer by the opaque of winter. Each necessitated the other, each followed and was followed. And Micah continued to walk through them, seeking only to nourish his soul in their union. He was content to pursue, content to travel, for with every experience he felt the City grow nearer to his soul. For The Divide would not end, it could not end, for it was to be his bridge to heaven.

And then, it was lost. Micah blinked, straining his eyes in the sun. The wind nudged his shoulder, but he did not answer. It waited patiently, but he would not speak to it. His throat ran dry, and his heart beat violently in his chest. He had accomplished that which he had long since forgotten. He had reached the end of The Divide.

Two halves met on a thin, sharp horizon. It bared no teeth, but was straight, taut as a lucky fisherman's line. One half was blue, a familiar sky that stretched above. The other was as yellow as the golden sun, and tossed like the tumultuous sea. Micah's mind locked, his heart stiffened, and his soul flushed in his veins. At first he saw nothing in the grass, but as he looked further, small cottages trailing contrails of smoke emerged. They sprinkled the yellow from the east to the west, tucked below the foothills and pushing fingers out to the horizon. A single discernable road ran between them, bisecting the vast floor, running from north to south. It was a valley, as far as the eye could see. A valley, brimming with grass that cupped the fire of the sun with an open palm. A valley, which burned in his mind like the valley that he had left so many seasons ago.

RETURN

The Divide watched wistfully as its child took his first uneasy steps in the valley below. It called him with wind, with sun, with the songs of birds and the gurgle of meltwater. But he did not stop, he did not hear its jealous call. Micah moved in a dream, for he did not believe his eyes. He did not trust his heart to beat, and he did not allow his soul to roam. He descended The Divide on an old trail beat into stone.

Micah thought very little when his feet touched the dirt of the low valley. He felt very little when his fingers ran along the sinews of grass. He could not respond to the first denizen he encountered, and only managed a weak greeting to the next. Though they shared a similar tongue he found that the words no longer came easily to his. He felt fear, he felt shame, but he still moved north, for it was all he had ever known. But in this place no voice whispered to him, no sensation courted his soul. He was confused; he was lost. He moved north, hoping for answers. He prayed, wishing the gods would respond. But as he passed through the villages, he came to realize that his prayers would not be answered. There was nothing in the northern horizon. The mountains that had occupied his late mind now scarred the south, although even these faded as he continued to walk. He walked for days, not knowing what he should find, not knowing what it was anymore that was deserving of his soul.

One day as he was walking the straight road north, he felt a familiar touch of wind over his ears. It came from behind, and as Micah turned, he realized that he could see nothing but tall grass all around him. Panic took hold, and he craned his neck to find the land that had once been his home. But it could not be found. There was only the same fluttering sea of yellow; the whisper of wind that passed through it. And Micah ran; he ran south in a frenzy, he did not stop to eat or to drink, nor did he seem to notice those who watched his frail body kicking up dust on the narrow road. He ran for his soul, for fear of losing it amidst the tall grass, for fear that he had abandoned it within The Divide.

The men and women of the valley watched as the ragged traveler stumbled and fell. They watched as he rose to his feet, only to fall again in a howl of agony. They watched him without pity as he wept in the dirt. And they were relieved when he dragged himself to the hill on the outskirts of their town. There he vanished, and the stir he had caused among them faded and died. But it was transitory, for word soon spread of a man yet alive on the hill. Some trained a suspicious eye to the site, and reported his doings to those that would hear them.

They watched as he gradually regained his footing, set about constructing a crude home, and began to shepherd the land with customs that to them were quite strange and yet proved productive. At first they despised him for his reclusiveness, for his apparent yield, and for his encroachment into the land they felt entitled to. But those who were not so proud sought his consult, for their families suffered and were hungry. When they brought his methods to their homesteads, they were rewarded with success. Even the proud eyes became hungry, and they too sought the man on the hill. He gave his knowledge readily, and they in turn welcomed him. But still he remained alone on his hill.

Legends and rumors began, and would catch with each new generation. His life was myth, but he was as real as the grass that grew beneath them. When the storms blew over the Southern Range he could be seen with his arms outstretched on the hillside. Those who dared to draw closer saw the light reflect in his open eyes, saw the fire dazzling in his face. They saw the lust in his eyes, but as the storm passed, it abated. He would wrinkle, stoop, and turn back to his home. And so he became a fixture of the land, constant between lives, so that children could not recall his entrance into their lands. To them he had lived atop the hill for an eternity, and would continue to do so.

But Micah did not forget his past. He learned to live in the new land, but always he felt he could not belong. In the evenings his young life called to him, but in his anger he did not answer its call. He was broken, he was betrayed. So he ignored his soul, and resigned himself to wither atop the lonely hill. He learned to enjoy its small comforts, he learned to live outside his soul. And The Divide remained on the horizon, and he remained on his hill, joined only by the straight and narrow road.

SEASONS

Dusk fell like the closing of a blanket, the crickets had begun to sing. A small breeze wafted lazily through the rivers of grass, drunken on the smell of pollen and dry earth that had become incumbent to the air. The sun slipped below the horizon, and only orange hues from the blinding of its lidless eye still bled into the night sky, riding the billowing cloud columns above. But even this light would be obscured by the shutter of night, and in time it evaporated from the sky leaving only a ceiling of cold darkness.

Micah stooped to break sticks from an ailing bush that had long toiled in his garden. He drew his pack closer, and added the sticks to a growing bundle, carefully binding them with cord fashioned from stalks of grass. Satisfied, he pulled the pack over his shoulders, and with his forehead bent to the earth shuffled along a little trail that burrowed through the yellow fields. Their stems brushed against his knees and their tufted heads tickled his cheeks as he passed. He smiled.

The trail bent upwards, gaining elevation slowly. The grass shortened, and Micah breathed heavily to maintain his pace on the trail. When he was out of breath he stopped, which was often. The stars had begun to emerge from the darkness above, and Micah pleased himself in his moments of rest to watch them sparkle. And when he walked he needed no light for the moon was full and served as a guide, the trail wriggled before his feet as a shadow between two shores illuminated under its glow.

But the stillness was broken when in the distant south a rumble shook the valley. Micah felt it deep within his bones, he felt it boiling the blood that ran in his veins, and he felt it knocking at the little box locked tightly within his chest. The smile left his face, replaced by a grimace. He did not take his eyes from the trail, but instead quickened his pace. From the south a crack whipped the air, followed by a roar. Micah tightened his jaw and moved quicker still. He loped up the hillside, slowed only by an unnatural gait in his left leg. A heavy knocking resonated in the earth, and Micah felt its

160

energy in his feet. He skipped as if stung, but did not break stride. He shuffled desperately until his meager home burst into view. But then he stopped, and the air around him held its breath.

He stopped, for he was no longer alone atop his hillside. Before his doorstep stood a little boy, whom with a tight knuckle struck at the home's fragile frame. The moonlight sparkled in his hair, and glowed on his skin. He did not see Micah approach, for his fit of anger was too great. And Micah was consumed by the boy, for his heart began to beat with old blood, and his mind receded deeply into his past. His lips tingled as he spoke, his arms were paralyzed by his sides. But the words managed to escape him.

"What are you doing here, what purpose do you have at my doorstep?"

Micah moved in a dream. The boy turned sharply, and scrutinized him with fierce eyes.

"Are you the one they call the Elder?" his small voice squeaked, "For I have a question for the one known as he!"

Micah blinked. He did not answer; his mind had become cavernously empty. The boy drew himself up before Micah, gripping the folds of his dirty trousers with his hands.

"Speak then, for I am the one who can answer," Micah could barely muster.

The boy smiled, and then stifled it with a frown before speaking. "Well you see, what I want to know is, what lies beyond the Southern Divide?"

Despite himself, Micah's eyes flickered to the horizon and held. The great ribcage of The Divide was lain open to the clouds which feasted from above, licking its bones with flashes of brilliant light. The valley shook with each strike, and the bones burned into his eyes with every bite that heaven took. He felt the box in his chest stir, as it always did when he beheld the domain of his youth. The place that had forsaken him back into the valley. The place that had left him with a starving soul.

"My son, could you not tell me what lies beyond those mountains?" Micah's words were weak like the wind that nuzzled his body.

The boy's face glowered, and his words escaped him without restraint. "But I don't believe it! My parents told me the stories of the City of the Gods, just like their parents did them. They told me about the great wonders, about the great Kings and Queens, about the white cloaks and their strange medicine. They told me about the Library of the Ages, and of its guardians: the keepers of its knowledge. I know of the temple, visited by the gods themselves; I have heard it all!"

"But you do not believe them? Why?"

The boy's frustration rose. "Because none of them have seen it! And of the travelers who have returned, some say that it does not exist! They say that there is nothing, nothing but another valley!"

Micah did not lift his eyes from the horizon. "And if they are right? If there is not a City beyond The Divide? Will you have this answer?"

The boy froze, his face fragile with confusion. "Have you ever been across The Divide?" He spoke in a reverent whisper, but his voice also betrayed a delicacy in the cracking of his notes.

The Divide flashed angrily, invitingly, beautifully. Micah wrested his eyes from it, and trained them on the boy. "My son, I have traveled far, I have seen many lands. But I wonder, what use are my words to you, one who has seen so little, one who desires so much? I am old, and you are young." His eyes abandoned the boy, and locked to the horizon. They were a dull gray in the moonlight. "My answer, what would they mean to such a youth?"

The boy scowled, and seeing his distraction muttered under his breath as he turned from Micah. He made for the trail down the hillside, and did not offer a single word of parting.

"Stop!" Micah's mind had begun to take hold as his heart shouted to wake him from his stupor. He saw the little boy halt and train an eye upon him, but not without a vestige of resentment. Micah felt himself alight in the glare, and loved the boy for it. Though his mouth ran dry and his mind still turned slowly, Micah felt his lips once again begin to move. He did not think the words as he spoke them, for they slipped

162

from the curtains of a place long forgotten, from memories that he no longer remembered. But his tongue recognized that voice, and there it was conceived into the wind.

"My child, I am sorry for not understanding. Though you are young, you have a lifetime ahead of you. Perhaps in time you will see. But if my age and long wandering have given me wisdom, it is that such questions must be answered. Do not deny them, do not ignore them. If they call you to go far, if they call you to strange and fearsome places, then listen. But still you are young, your guide is not true. Beware the long journey, beware The Divide. Though along it you may find your answer, remember that by pain are the answers revealed. Remember this if your passion takes you there, and remember that not only by its trail might the City be found. If you are careful, if you are wise, then you might find the answers much closer to your heart. For your sake child, I hope that you do."

There was silence in the vacuum that followed. Micah's features tightened, for the words had broken beyond his restraint, released without question. But he did not return them, and instead waited with uncertainty as the boy twisted to see him, producing an inquisitive face. "By what other trail might I find it?"

His eyes shone with desperation, with relentless drive and aspiration. His chest moved quickly, his mouth open subtly in effort disguise his hopeful breaths. He looked to Micah, open to his wisdom, open to instruction, with passion that awaited a simple arrow of guidance.

But Micah could not answer. He waited for the words to resurface, but found there were none. He stood, wrinkled and grey, stooping by the weight of the load on his back, withering atop the gentle hill. His knees shook and his face quivered, and still his mind waited for his soul to answer. But it was bound to the box inside his chest, where he had locked it before stepping into the valley. And although it clanged to escape, it was too late, for the boy saw that he had no answer.

The boy's face sank into shadow. "So there is only one path," he resigned.

Micah flustered, but before the boy could return to the trail burst out once more, for he needed desperately to have a single question answered. "What is your name, my son?"

The boy faced the trail, but he threw a last glance over his shoulder. His eyes burned, scorching Micah as they crossed his own. "My name is Giralt." And then Giralt descended into the shadows.

Micah stared at the space he had occupied. Two small tracks remained, darkened by their impressions in the moonlit soil. They did not vanish; they did not blow away in the wind.

"By the gods, do my senses betray me?" Micah whispered. His face was pale, white as the moon that sailed across the night sky. Micah pried his eyes from the footprints, and let them wander to meet the faces he knew above. "Is he to cross The Divide as I have? Am I here to be its messenger to him?" But the stars did not answer. Instead the south rumbled, and a brilliant burst of light lit the corners of his eyes.

He stood at the end of his hill, overlooking the Southern Divide, as the wind began to whistle through the thistle and weeds. His coat flapped as it swelled and then washed over the hillside. The dirt that it carried stung his eyes, but he did not notice. For to the south The Divide marched its Knights along the horizon, each engaged in its penance with the lashings of heaven, thrashing and convulsing as holy fire burst over their mighty shoulders. They tossed and roared as they received their beatings, some standing taller than their brothers, others stooping low in defeat.

Tears welled in Micah's eyes. His wooden features softened, and his old body shook. Micah fell to his knees. He spoke, and the words were agony to his aged throat. "Why did it end, was there no more it could show me? This place is pain, this place is still, this place has no beauty. Surely it is not the way to the City, surely it is not one of its faces? My soul, you betrayed me. You led me north; you led me into this abyss; how now could I trust you?"

The box rattled in his chest, and with every flash of The Divide it struck against its walls. Micah groaned, and his voice rose in its plea. "If it is not north, then how does one seek the

City? Where then do we learn its faces, where then do we glimpse at its beauty?"

The Divide howled in the night, and its tempest grew. Along the horizon its lights did not cease, and Micah felt the pressure rise in his chest with each mighty blow. "Would you have me follow you once more? Would you tempt me again into the wilderness, to desire the summit, to revel once more in fear and in beauty?"

Micah lifted his left leg with great effort. "I am no longer young. I am no longer capable. Such beauty is so far from me now; it was taken from me by your hands." The wind whirled across Micah's body, and he staggered to retain balance. "My soul, again I have nothing. Again I am lost, for without your guidance there can be no beauty. Tell me, is there another trail to the City? What face have I ignored?" Tears worked down the channels of his cheeks, and his voice rose to a shout as the wind rushed down the canal of his throat. "I ask you, I beg you again, what face have I ignored? I wish to see you once more, but my weary soul, I do not know how!"

The Divide continued to roar. But as Micah wept bitterly, the mountains revealed themselves in the clouds, for as the flashes multiplied the horizon began to take form. No longer did each Knight stand alone, but his brother stood beside him, locked in the same struggle, bearing the same punishment, and yet each thrusting its head high. The low saddles joined them at their shoulders, and upon each other they withstood the torment. Micah's eyes widened as he saw a youth sprout from the neck of his father, saw a mother cradle its small children within a cirque of her towers, saw a brother supporting the annihilated face of his twin. He saw as The Divide was connected, sharing in their punishments, sharing in their triumph, sharing in their joys. And he felt a bitter longing as the key turned and his soul once more filled his fingertips.

Not all that stood in The Divide shared the ridgeline. One summit stood alone, rotten and black, torn by the hands of the gods, still raising its ugly head to the heaven to be smote by its hand. There it knew glory, there it knew pain, and it there knew the brightest day and the darkest night. "I know your summit," Micah whispered. "Where is your father?

Where is your mother? Where is your sister? Are they still there, waiting for you? Do you still wait for them? You have known fear, you have known pain, you have known power and you have known joy. You knew them within one another, and by it you grew. Why then are you alone? Why did you stop, when you found beauty? Were you not once told, that beauty has many faces?"

Micah looked south, and before him the light that flashed on the horizon coalesced into one. It beat with the rhythm of his heart, a low throb that he felt from his hands and into his toes. He felt the ground shake and saw the sky burst, he saw the grass quiver and jump and felt the wind stagger and blow. He watched as the clouds slipped back behind the wall, and carried the light with them. They spilled across The Divide like water, filling the low valleys and bursting over high passes. They rode the high shoulders of the White Mountain, and entrenched the feet of the Knights in the Hall. They spanned The Divide, carrying the holy fire with them, but in The Divide they would not remain. Pushed south with the wind, they built on the dam of the Twisted Peak, and finally collapsed over the Three Finger Pass with a tremendous splash. The clouds took the light south, and from behind The Divide the light remained, fading, bursting, fragmenting the night sky, splitting it into day. It hung over fields of yellow, over homes nestled into the dirt, and over an old tree bent low by the seasons. And then suddenly, as it had begun, the beating stopped. The horizon was silent once more.

And Micah moved south, as only his soul still knew how.

Made in the USA
Middletown, DE
09 March 2017